EVERGREEN

A WILLIE BLACK MYSTERY

EVERGREEN
HOWARD OWEN

THE PERMANENT PRESS
Sag Harbor, NY 11963

For information, address:
  The Permanent Press
  4170 Noyac Road
  Sag Harbor, NY 11963
  www.thepermanentpress.com

Library of Congress Cataloging-in-Publication Data

  Owen, Howard, author.
    Evergreen / Howard Owen.
    Sag Harbor, NY: The PermanenT Press, [2019]
    Series: A Willie Black mystery
    ISBN: 978-1-57962-573-3
      1. Mystery fiction.

  PS3565.W552 E94 2019
  813'.54—dc23   2019003024

Printed in the United States of America

To Karen

CHAPTER ONE

Monday, January 1, 2018

New Year's Day seldom finds me in a festive mood. It's more like post-festive. I yearn for the time when I could pass out at three A.M. and sleep like a baby until some decent hour in the early afternoon.

Instead I wake up at eight fifteen, perhaps because the damn cat is standing on my chest. I know rolling over and going back to sleep is a nonstarter. Butterball is lightly batting my face as a gentle reminder that, even though my head feels like a piñata and there's a party hat dangling by a string from my neck, her majesty must be fed. I didn't tell you to chug cheap bubbly, those accusing feline eyes a few inches away tell me.

Plus, my back hurts and I have to piss like a racehorse.

Cindy is gently snoring beside me. Her head is sticking out of one of the leg holes of a pair of men's underpants, hopefully mine. My fourth and final wife seems to have convinced the cat that I am her go-to servant for early morning necessities. I resist the urge to wake the blushing bride.

It is smart, in a dumb-ass kind of way, to host New Year's Eve parties. That way, you don't have to dodge police roadblocks or call Uber or Lyft. All we had to manage was the route to the master bedroom after the last guest mercifully left.

Looking at the bomb that seems to have gone off in our living room, though, I can see the wisdom in getting a hotel room next year. Empty bottles of faux-champagne, slobber-coated party horns and cheap plastic plates are everywhere. I gawk in wonder at our soup bowls, crusted with some gray shit that looks like hardening cement. And then I remember. The goddamn black-eyed peas. Patti Garland across the hall brought them sometime after midnight for good luck. Good luck getting invited if we ever do this again, Patti.

Butterball has followed me, padding down the hall and mewing as if I might forget why I'm up at this ungodly hour. Then the phone rings.

I am on the hook to work New Year's Day on the night cops beat, but my shift won't start for about six more hours. Please, I'm thinking as I check the number, don't let the carnage have started already. Let me have a few hours before the city's criminals start trying to top last year's impressive sixty-seven murders. Let my city (and me) rest a little longer.

I don't recognize the number, so it isn't anyone at the paper. And it's too early for the scammers. I pick up and answer, in my most accommodating tone, "What?"

There's a pause, and I think for a second that it is some kind of robo-call, my first of the year. I'm about to hang up when I hear a voice on the other end that I recognize faintly.

"Willie?"

I affirm that he has indeed reached the Black residence.

"It's Richard Slade."

Not someone I expected to hear from. I don't think he's ever called me at home before.

"Sorry, Richard. I'm still kind of easing into the day. Didn't mean to be cranky."

Richard Slade once did nearly half a lifetime for a rape he didn't commit, and he almost spent the other half in prison for a murder that also was done by someone else. In my never-ending quest for truth, justice, and cheap-ass Virginia Press Association awards, I helped keep that from happening, so we do have some history.

And, oh yeah, he's my cousin, somewhat removed.

"I wouldn't have called this early, but Momma insisted. She wants to see you."

"Now?"

"Well, she's not doing so good, Willie."

I hear Richard's voice crack a little and then he clears his throat the way men do when they don't want other men to know they're about to lose it.

"She's down here at MCV. It's her heart, they think. It don't look good, Willie."

I tell him I'll be there as soon as I can make myself a cup of coffee. A Camel or two on the way is in the offing too. "Stop smoking" was not one of my New Year's resolutions.

I wonder why Philomena Slade, Richard's long-suffering mother, wants to see her first cousin once removed on a day when she has more important things to consider, like trying to stay alive. It seems rude to ask.

Richard anticipates my confusion.

"She said she wanted to tell you something, something about Artie. She said it was important."

"I'll be right there."

The coffee can wait.

CHAPTER TWO

Artie is—or was—Artie Lee. He and I share some history, too, or at least some DNA.

He was my father, the dad I never had.

He died before I was talking. I have almost no memory of him. He and Peggy never got married, mostly because I was born seven years before the Supreme Court forced the Commonwealth of Virginia to let African Americans and white folks marry each other.

Even after they didn't have a non-Caucasian adult male around to remind them of their grandson's provenance, Peggy's parents pretty much put my mother and me on the missing-persons list.

Peggy has never talked much about Artie, and I have to admit that he hasn't crossed my mind in some time. He is an abstraction, an absence I never really felt. Judging from the quality of the bastards who lived with my mother intermittently when I was growing up, the lack of a male presence in your childhood is not a fate worse than death.

Artie Lee has been a closed book to me, one I never had any great urge to open. So why the hell does Philomena Slade suddenly want to tell me something about my dear old dad?

Richard said "MCV," but he meant Virginia Commonwealth University Medical Center. Hell, they only changed the name fourteen years ago. We don't embrace change here in Richmond, where holding back the hands of time is a twenty-four-hour-a-day job.

The hospital parking deck is as empty as it ever gets. It's still a few minutes shy of ten o'clock, a tad early for visitors, especially on New Year's Day.

I only get lost once trying to find the area of the complex where they're trying to save Philomena. I do manage to grab a cup of coffee along the way.

Richard comes to get me in the visitors' area and takes me through the maze I'll need help extricating myself from, and finally we come to his mother's room.

They brought Philomena in by ambulance last night. I can imagine what a clusterfuck that must have been. New Year's Eve at the emergency room of a big teaching hospital is twenty-first-century bedlam. I've had to come here three or four times over the years as a reporter when festive mayhem erupted into fatalities.

Richard says they've given her all kinds of tests, and then she spent half the night waiting for a room to open up here in the intensive-care ward.

She looks tired, and about ten years older than the last time I saw her, which, I'm ashamed to admit, was more than a year ago.

She's sleeping when I come in, but as I take a seat beside her bed, she opens her eyes.

"Willie," she says weakly. She thanks me for coming. She asks me about Cindy, whose name she remembers despite the fact that she's only met her once, and then about Peggy, whom she's known since before I was born.

I answer her questions and wait for her to get to the point. She's got a tube stuck in her nose and has to time her words with her breathing.

"I want you to do something for me," she says finally, taking hold of my hand. Her grip, despite her diminished condition and the fact that she can't weigh much more than one hundred pounds, is strong. It is the grip of a woman who spent the better part of thirty years fighting like hell to get her son out of prison when everybody else thought he was guilty as sin.

"I want you to go out to Evergreen," she says. "I want you to take care of Artie's grave."

I nod my head, dumb as a post.

"I've been doing it up till now," she says, "but I don't know if I'm going to be able to keep it up."

She turns toward me, her near-death clutch entrapping my wrist.

"It's a terrible thing," she says, "to be forgotten. I don't want Artie Lee to be forgotten."

I nod my head like I know what the hell she's talking about.

Then a tiny bulb lights up inside my hungover brain.

Evergreen. Evergreen Cemetery. I've never been there, but we've done stories about it in the newspaper. It's somewhere on the eastern edge of the city, out in that no-man's land between the projects and the country. The story I remember was about trying to save it. Whoever started Evergreen must have walked off after they filled it with graves, leaving it to the deceased's families to take care of it. Some did, but according to the article I remember, most didn't, and the place was a holy mess. Volunteers could only do so much.

"Artie's buried at Evergreen?"

Her eyes widen.

"You didn't know that? You didn't know where your father was buried?"

It is an accusation I accept without protesting that he was my father in name only.

Philomena sighs.

"I don't suppose Peggy told you much about him. She didn't come around after he was killed, and I reckon she was just as happy to put Artie Lee behind her."

She hasn't let go of my wrist yet.

"You've got to know something though," she says. "They really did love each other. It just wasn't the right time. Folks were mean about things like that back then. But love don't see color. At least it didn't for them."

Then she lets go. Her head falls back on her pillow, and I'm wondering if I've just heard Philomena Slade's last words. Richard stands like he's going to run for a nurse. But then she opens her eyes again.

"One more thing I'd like to ask you to do," she says. "I want you to talk to Arthur. Arthur Meeks. Get him to tell you about Artie. Him and Artie were close. He can tell you what you need to know."

Then she closes her eyes. Richard gets a nurse, who comes in and assures him that his mother is resting, not resting in peace.

I lean over and give her a kiss on her forehead. It just seems like the thing to do.

Richard walks me back down to the floor where we can both grab a little breakfast. Richard says he hasn't eaten since "sometime yesterday afternoon."

He happened to be at his mother's when the chest pains she'd been having for a couple of hours finally got bad enough for her to mention them.

"She didn't want me to call an ambulance, just wanted me to drive her over there, but I knew she'd get more attention if the EMTs brought her in."

He eats a breakfast sandwich and I nibble on what passes for a bagel in a Richmond hospital. He brings me up to speed on Artie Lee's grave.

My father died in 1961, and for "maybe twenty years" Artie's mother would go out there and cut back the weeds twice a year. Other relatives joined her, including Philomena.

"Those old folks, they used to treat it like a picnic," Richard says between bites. "They'd take fried chicken and potato salad and sweet tea and such out there and make a day of it. And they'd clean off the grave site and talk about who was buried there."

When Artie's mother, the grandmother I never met, got too old to keep it up, Philomena took over.

"I helped her a few times, after I got out," he says. "It seemed like it meant a lot to her. Man, when I'm done, I want 'em to just cremate my ass and scatter my ashes, maybe up in the mountains somewhere."

I prefer the outfield at the Diamond with maybe a little bit sprinkled underneath the back table at Joe's Inn, but to each his own.

Richard says Evergreen is a mess now.

"The place where Artie's buried, it's all overgrown with weeds and ivy and all. Some kids were out there with sling blades last time I went out with her, trying to clear the underbrush, but it looked like pissin' in the wind to me."

He says his mother probably went there the last time sometime before Christmas "to put flowers on Artie's grave."

He gives me a look.

"Maybe I can help you some, with the grave and all," he says. It is unspoken but understood that the primary onus here ought to fall on Artie Lee's son.

Richard stands. He says he needs to get back upstairs.

"Before you go," I say, "who was that guy your mother said to talk to. Arthur somebody?"

"Oh. Arthur Meeks. Momma said him and Artie Lee used to hang out together. I don't know what Arthur Meeks could tell you about anything though. He must be about eighty. I don't think he's doing all that well. I took Momma to see him one day a couple of years ago I think it was. He lives somewhere over there in eastern Henrico, around Sandston."

I digest half the bagel and leave the rest. I think Joe's is open on New Year's Day. I hope to hell so. I need some grease.

—m—

I RETURN to the Prestwould before noon. The twelve-story high-rise where Cindy and I rent our sixth-floor digs from my most-recent ex-wife is still easing into the new year. The lobby is almost empty, and I wish it were emptier, because Feldman, aka McGrumpy, my least-favorite Prestwouldian, is sitting in a chair across from the south tower elevator.

He lives to complain. He has been threatening to sell his unit for as long as I've known him, but he never does. Several of the more affluent residents here have actually talked about buying him out, just to get his gossipy, mean-spirited ass out of here. Hell, he'd never sell. He's having too much fun.

"Can you believe they haven't cleaned up yet from the party?" he says by way of greeting.

I guess he means the Christmas party. Yes, a tree and some other decorations from the Prestwould's annual fete still adorn the lobby.

"I'm going to have to speak to that girl about this. Where is she anyhow? It's almost twelve o'clock."

"That girl" would be Marcia, the manager of our little asylum. She's in her early thirties and has been here at least six years.

"It's New Year's Day," I remind Feldman.

"We give her New Year's Day off? With pay?" McGrumpy asks. "What's next, Arbor Day?"

The elevator mercifully arrives. As I depart, I tell Feldman I hope he gets everything he deserves in 2018.

Cindy has managed in my absence to not only rouse herself and lose the boxers she was wearing the last time I saw her but also to clean up about two-thirds of the party tornado.

"Well, you picked a fine time to flee the premises," she says. "Can we sue the Garlands for bringing the black-eyed peas?"

I tell her I'll check with Marcus Green the next time I talk with my favorite ambulance-chaser.

"This is the last time we serve drinks that aren't see-through," she mutters as she examines a Rorschach blot of red wine by the dining-room table.

"Where were you, by the way?"

I explain the call from Richard Slade and all the particulars of my visit to the hospital.

"You mean you've never seen your father's grave?"

"Didn't know he had one. Hey, cut me some slack. I can't even remember him. Some people didn't grow up in Ozzie and Harriet land. Lots of kids on the Hill didn't even know who their fathers were."

"Well," Cindy says, "all your pathetic self-pitying aside, I still think you ought to have tried to find out something about the man."

"High moral ground," I observe, "for someone who, when I last saw her, was wearing some man's underpants around her neck."

Cindy shrugs.

"Maybe I shouldn't drink so much. And anyhow, they probably were yours."

"Probably?"

She grins and asks me if Joe's is open.

—ɯ—

"By the way," she asks as we're waiting for the elevator, "what was his full name?"

"Who?"

"Your father, you knucklehead. Artie Lee can't be all of it."

"Hell if I know."

"You never asked Peggy?"

"Not that I can remember."

She sighs.

"I would write it off to you being a man, but even among that deplorable subset, you lower the average."

McGrumpy is still there when we reach the first floor. Mercifully, he is busy enumerating his complaints to another unfortunate neighbor. We make our escape.

Not that I'd admit it, but Cindy could be right. For an alleged hard-nosed reporter, I have been somewhat negligent, family tree-wise. It's never seemed important to me to trace my roots back to Charlemagne. As far as names go, "Artie Lee" always seemed like name enough for me. I mean, I'm just Willie, not William.

Willie Mays Black, I guess because Peggy thought naming me for an African American baseball player would drive her parents even crazier than the particulars of my birth had driven them already.

I really ought to talk with my dear old marijuana-muddled mom about Artie Lee, I guess.

"So Philomena Slade wants you to take over tending your late father's grave. That's kind of sweet, I think."

Kind of sweaty is more like it, I observe.

"I'll help you," she says.

Cindy called R.P. McGonnigal and Andy Peroni, her brother, on the way over. She and I are able to get the big back table and hold it while we wait for them.

"It seems strange, without Abe," she says as we study the menus we already know by heart.

I nod in agreement. Abe Custalow still has a bed in our place, but he hasn't been around for a while. I hope there's not too much water over the goddamn dam to save a lifetime of friendship.

R.P. and Andy arrive just as a party of six is giving us the stink-eye for hogging the big table. We saw my old Oregon Hill pals only a few hours ago, at the party. R.P. hasn't combed his hair today, and Andy has his shirt tucked inside his underwear. R.P. has brought along the guy he's currently living with, whose name is either Matt or Mack and works blocking city streets for FedEx.

"You all sure know how to give a party," R.P. says as we tuck into the three-buck-fifty Bloody Marys and order food.

Cindy notes that we might have to pare the guest list next time.

"What?" her brother says. "We were gentlemen throughout."

"Guilty dog barks," Cindy says. "I seem to recall seeing someone who looked a lot like you two flicking black-eyed peas at each other. That crap is still stuck to the wall."

"It must have been somebody else. There's a lot of people that look like me. Plus, you were too drunk to be a reliable witness.

"Besides," he says, pointing at R.P., "he started it."

Our food comes, and Cindy tells them about my visit to the hospital this morning.

"You don't know where he's buried?" Andy says.

"I do now, sort of."

"Hell," R.P. says, "now that you mention it, I'm not so sure where my old man is planted. After him and Mom split, we sort of lost touch."

I turn to Cindy.

"See. I rest my case. I am not the only guy who doesn't know where his father's grave is."

She mutters something about birds of a feather as R.P. and I high-five.

—⟋⟍⟍—

THE NEWSROOM is quiet. It's almost as if my compatriots also stayed up to greet the new year. Hell, I know a few of them did.

Chip Grooms drops by my desk to comment on the quality of the festivities.

"There was some woman there with a pair of men's underpants on her head," he says.

Sarah Goodnight is sitting at her desk, although slouching might be a better term. She must be concentrating on something really important, because her eyes are closed.

I tiptoe in and greet her, perhaps more loudly than necessary.

She comes out of her reverie, banging her knee on the desk.

"Jesus Christ, Willie. Don't you ever knock?"

I ask her what great journalism we're going to foist on our readers tomorrow.

"What do you think?" she says, waving across the slumbering newsroom. "Thank God for the Associated Press."

Sarah's an editor now. She's probably a good one, although it's hard to tell. Editors only get noticed when things get fucked up. But, as I've explained to her more than once, they don't get laid off as often as reporters, and the hours are better.

I ask her if she has a city map.

She reaches behind her and hands me one.

"Why don't you just Google it?" she says.

I tell her that I have a soft spot in my heart for print.

I search for a few minutes before I finally find what I'm looking for. Evergreen Cemetery. It's a little green blot not far from a bigger green blot. Not far off Nine Mile Road, it looks like. The dead have a great view of I-64 East.

"What are you looking for?" Sarah asks me.

"My father."

She takes a sip of her coffee.

"Wait. Isn't your father, like, dead? Like a long time ago?"

"That's what they tell me."

"So . . ."

I tell her I'm looking for his grave. She opens her mouth to ask me what everybody else has been asking me.

"Don't start," I advise.

I leave her to her contemplations.

Sally Velez wants me to check with the police to see if anybody got killed overnight. Some cities tout the first baby born in the new year. Here, we're waiting for the first stiff.

Nobody knows anything at cop headquarters. Nobody would know anything if half of Gilpin Court had murdered the other half. Keeping things from the news media is a way of life among our men and women in blue. My only reliable source, Peachy Love, has the day off.

We do get a tip that somebody crashed a party somewhere in the near West End and relieved the guests of many of their valuables. The guests, though no doubt drunk, were sensible enough to know that stuff is less important than life, so nobody was injured. Still, it'll probably make a good cautionary tale for tomorrow's paper if I can chase it down. Well-off white folks getting robbed, maybe by minorities, always sells papers.

There's plenty of time on this mercifully quiet night to do some more searching. I find that there are three "A. Meeks" entries in the city directory. One lives on North Side, one is a woman. The third, who appears to live out near the airport, seems to be the best bet to be Arthur Meeks.

I jot down the phone number and address and promise myself that I'll pay the man a visit sometime soon. It's probably a fool's errand, but I did promise Philomena Slade, and she's a tough old broad who will haunt me from the grave if I don't follow through.

CHAPTER THREE

Tuesday

The New Year's Eve home invasion story made it to A1 this morning, below the fold.

"I just don't know what gets into people," the lady of the house said when I found her and her husband last night soaking their bruised egos with bourbon-and-waters. "I mean, they were so rude. F-word this and F-word that. It just ruined the evening."

Ruin, I wanted to tell her, is relative. The husband said he wished he'd had his trusty Glock at hand instead of upstairs in the bedside table. I resisted the urge to tell him he's probably lucky he didn't.

—⁂—

I CALL Richard Slade for an update. He tells me that his mother is "hanging in there." I ask if I can stop by and see her. He says that'd be fine, although she might not be up for talking much.

I don't really need for her to talk much. What I need is directions.

Philomena is resting when I come in. I can't make much sense of the numbers on all the machines she's hooked up to, but I sense that the future's not bright.

Philomena is one of those people who remind me of the Jimmy Stewart character in *It's A Wonderful Life*. If she'd never been born, the world surely would be a sadder place.

For one thing, Richard probably would be in prison for most of the rest of his life without a mother who nagged and nagged until somebody checked out the DNA and found out that, oops, they'd locked up the wrong guy.

Plus, she's been pretty much raising her great-nephews, Jeroy and Jamal, so her niece, Chanelle, can finish school.

When she's not keeping the graves of long-forgotten family members clean, she's hauling every person older than herself to doctors' offices and grocery shopping for them.

Philomena Slade, when she passes on, will be missed.

Richard tells me to keep it brief.

I lean down. She looks up at me, smiles, and croaks out a hello.

"Philomena," I say, taking her hand. "I need to know where my father is buried. I mean, where in Evergreen."

As little as I know about the place, I know it's a jungle in there—thousands of graves and no map.

"Just go to Maggie Walker," she says after a pause. "It's right down the hill from there. Just past it, maybe fifty yards."

I know, more or less, what she means. Maggie Walker was one of those people who should be more famous than she is. First woman banker in the United States, no mean feat considering that she was an African American born in Richmond in the dying days of the Civil War.

They've finally erected a monument to her, over in front of one of my favorite restaurants just off Broad Street. In classic Richmond fashion, preservationists opposed the site because they had to cut down a bleeping live oak to make room for her in the little pocket park.

The statue is not as fancy as those Civil War behemoths on Monument Avenue, but you have to start somewhere, don't you?

I knew she was buried at Evergreen. So now all I have to do is find Maggie and Artie can't be far behind.

Philomena is asleep as I slip out. Richard and I have a cup of coffee. He tells me the doctors aren't terribly optimistic.

"Well," I tell him, "they don't know what a tough lady your momma is."

"Don't know where I'd be without her. Well, yeah, I do. You and her, you saved me."

OK, it does make me feel good to see a decent man set free, but anything I did just falls under the heading of being a nosy-ass reporter.

—ɯ—

Peggy's at home when I stop by. Seeing Philomena the way she looked at the hospital makes me realize that my mother isn't going to be around forever either. She'll be seventy-six this year, still stoned about half the time. What the fuck, she doesn't bother anybody, she manages to pay her bills with whatever little bit she saved in her blue-collar working life plus Social Security and a little help now and then from me and Cindy. If they aren't going to legalize pot for everybody, they ought to at least legalize it for people who are too damn old to enjoy much of anything else.

When she took in Awesome Dude a few years ago, it looked like an act of charity to me, but it has turned into a good deal for her. Awesome fetches her groceries and takes her to the doctor, usually driving the beat-up old Ford Galaxy we got for her. Awesome doesn't have a driver's license, of course, but we keep hoping that won't become an issue. And his Social Security and other benefits he gets for basically being unable to adjust his weird self to workaday life, plus a small inheritance he got from his family in exchange for staying away from them, help pay the bills.

Peggy doesn't look like she's almost seventy-six. Maybe marijuana has antiaging properties. This early in the day, she's pretty coherent, with maybe just a breakfast toke under her belt.

I tell her about Philomena.

"That's terrible," she says. "I need to get over and see her. God, it's been years."

When I tell her what Philomena asked me to do, Peggy gets quiet.

"Yeah," she says finally, "I know where it is."

"Evergreen Cemetery?"

"His grave."

This is news to me.

As a kid, I'd ask about my father and Peggy would just brush me off, tell me that he died in a car accident, and that she didn't want to talk about it.

As a younger adult, I tried a couple of times to draw her out on the subject of Artie Lee. The last time, after Peggy felt like I'd gone from inquiring to pestering, she told me to leave well-enough alone and not ask her about it anymore.

"We was just kids. We didn't even know each other that well," she said. "He wouldn't have been here to raise you even if he had lived. It wasn't like we could of got married or anything."

She said she didn't know anything about the wreck.

"They just called me, an aunt or something, and said he was dead. And that was it."

Now, though, seems like the time to press a little harder.

"So you've been to his grave site? When? Why didn't you tell me?"

She shrugs.

"I didn't see any sense in it. Artie Lee is finished business. Just leave it alone."

"But you've been out there."

She sighs.

"Hell, I wish I'd never mentioned it. Yeah, I've been a few times, now and then."

"How long since you've been there?"

"I don't know," she says. "Maybe a couple of years. The place was right much of a mess."

Why, I ask her again, didn't she let me in on any of this?

My mother, a hard case from way back, seems to be about to cry.

"It wasn't something I was proud of," she says. "Damn, Willie, you've got to know what it was like back then. It was just better if I moved on."

"But you've been going to his grave."

"So maybe I'm not as good at forgetting as I'd like to be. So shoot me."

She slams a Miller can down on the coffee table, making it foam over the side, and walks over to the sink, full of unwashed breakfast dishes.

I walk over behind her and put my arms around her from behind.

"Well, you're going back to Evergreen, and you're going to take me. You're going to show me Artie Lee's grave."

She tries to get away. I hang on tight.

"Wasn't I a good enough parent for you?" she says. "Why do you want to dig up Artie Lee now?"

I tell her that I don't mean to literally dig him up now. I remind her that I have been given the solemn duty of keeping Artie's grave clean for all eternity or until I can find another sucker to take over that august responsibility.

"And how am I going to do that, how am I going to keep my promise to Philomena if I can't even find the damn grave?" No sense in telling her that Philomena has already given me directions.

We go back into the living room and sit, neither of us saying anything for a while.

Finally, Peggy looks up, a little teary-eyed.

"OK," she says.

"OK, you'll come with me?"

"What the hell do you think I mean?"

I tell my mother, as I haven't told her enough, that she was all the parent I ever needed or wanted.

"But I just want to know."

"Know what?"

"I don't know. Something. Anything."

Philomena asking me to clean his grave, plus the reaction by everyone when they realized I didn't know where my own father was buried, has awakened my curiosity. My curiosity is a dangerous thing. Like Butterball, it constantly demands to be fed.

Hell, I'm not like those folks who spend their waking hours on Ancestry.com. I don't need to know when my six-times great-grandfather came to America, whether it was on the Mayflower or a slave ship.

I would, though, like to be able to trace my roots back at least one generation. Is that asking too much?

We agree that I'll pick her up tomorrow morning at nine for a trip to Evergreen.

—⁓—

CINDY'S BACK molding young minds, so the place is empty when I run by for lunch before going to the paper. I feed Butterball, and by the time I'm through making myself a grilled cheese sandwich and washing it down with a beer, the cat is begging again. I turn up the sound on the Delbert McClinton CD just to drown out her piteous mewing.

Often on a day like this, Custalow would come up for his lunch break and we'd talk about the boiler or the Redskins or some other guy thing.

Abe does have his job back, I'm happy to say, overseeing the care of our creaky 1920s vintage building. A brief incarceration for murder caused the management company to can him, but when it turned out that he was innocent, they offered him his old job. They might not have made the offer if Marcus Green, lawyer extraordinaire, hadn't hinted at legal repercussions.

Abe regained his freedom and lost his only son, all in one fell swoop. My role in that rather Biblical denouement has my oldest friend and former roommate keeping his distance these days. We speak when we run into each other in the lobby, but things aren't the same. He doesn't go to Joe's to drink and tell lies with us anymore.

He is for the time being residing with the lovely Stella Stellar. Cindy and I miss the rent money he contributed every month. We miss him too.

—⁓—

After an hour spent shooting pool at Greenleaf's, I make my way to the paper. I avoid the siren call of Penny Lane, just around the corner. It was cruel of God to put a pool hall and an excellent British pub within a stone's throw of where I work.

I crush the Camel I've been nursing for two blocks and enter the realm of MediaWorld.

We used to think we had it bad, when the local ownership started slicing and dicing what once was a proud daily rag. We screamed bloody murder when they started trimming the width of the paper to save money on newsprint. We pissed and moaned when ads started showing up in places where ads never were before, like on section fronts. We wondered what the hell the suits were thinking when they started giving away "content," meaning the shit that was in that day's paper, to our Internet readers. We mourned the loss of Christmas bonuses and raises.

Then came MediaWorld, which taught us that the old Joni Mitchell song was right. You really don't know what you've got until it's fucking gone.

MediaWorld bought the paper after the local guys, who seem like Mother Teresa now, took out some loans they couldn't repay fast enough to please the bank. MW, as it calls itself, has made two rounds of layoffs in the last two years, with no promise that more aren't on the way. It has all but gutted the features section and depends on other MW papers and the wire services for most of what fills our pages. The paper's so thin now that we wonder when they'll stop publishing every day. The smart money is on Tuesday to be the first to go.

They also send us another publisher every year or so, and none of them, to my knowledge, has ever been to a baseball game at the Diamond, taken the footbridge across the James to Belle Isle, or eaten at Mamma Zu's. They tend to buy houses as far out in the suburbs as they can and still get to work downtown in the morning.

The last one left in a hurry, announcing all of a sudden that he was going to "pursue other interests." Yeah, like maybe finding some other bunch of idiots who won't vet his résumé before they hire him.

So now we have Benson Stine, or B.S. as we fondly refer to him out of his hearing range.

Benson Stine looks like he's about twenty-five, but everybody under forty looks like a kid to me these days, as I'm sure everyone over forty gets typecast by B.S. and his peers under the general heading of "decrepit."

He's actually thirty-five, I've learned. They sent him here from Des Moines, and he understands Richmond as well as you might expect from someone hailing from Des Moines. He doesn't like steamed blue crabs, doesn't understand why beach music is a thing, and isn't quite straight on which one was Stuart, which one was Jackson, and which one was Lee, as well as why those big-ass monoliths are out there on Monument Avenue.

And, like all publishers, he wants to leave his imprint.

Recently he's left his imprint on my ass, in the form of a little feature called "This Day in Richmond History."

In the not-so-distant past, this is the kind of crap, if done at all, that would have been performed by an intern or some freelancer, or by our library. We don't have interns though. Some geniuses high in Media-World decided those $12-an-hour student journalists were a frivolous expense. The same brain trust ruled that we had to cut our stringer budget to almost zero. And the powers that be decided years ago that we didn't really need a library to keep photos and stories in some kind of order.

Thus, when someone like Benson Stine decides that the paper should run a short feature *every bleeping day* about something that happened on that particular date sometime in Richmond's long and sordid history, some hapless staffer has to step up to the plate and take a high, hard one.

I got beaned a couple of weeks ago.

Stine called me to his office the week before Christmas. I was pretty sure he wasn't doing it to wish me Happy Holidays or tell me the company had reinstituted bonuses. There weren't any rumors of upcoming layoffs, and a newsroom full of reporters usually sniffs that kind of shit out well before the ax falls. So I was in the dark when Sandy McCool told me her boss would see me, and to let myself in.

I did not expect good news. I was not disappointed.

Stine, who has lost hair and gained pounds at an alarming rate, to judge from the college-age picture that sits on his desk, motioned me to have a seat.

It was the first time we'd met one-on-one. If I never have to meet a publisher one-on-one again, it'll be too soon. It almost never works to your advantage to have a tête-a-tête with someone to whom you can't safely say "no."

He called me "Mr. Black." As I age, the "Mr." sounds more and more like code for "old, doddering dinosaur, when are you going to retire?"

I told him "Willie" would be fine.

"Willie," he said, "I have an exciting opportunity for you."

Oh, shit, I thought. An opportunity.

The opportunity gifted to me was the chance to write a piece *every bleeping day* about something noteworthy that happened on that date in some year since the English reached these parts in 1607, about a minute and a half after they landed at Jamestown.

I hemmed and hawed a bit, showing all the enthusiasm I could manufacture for the publisher's fine idea while gently suggesting that my dance card was already pretty full.

"Oh," B.S. said, "I'm sure someone with your talent and experience can find time. This can't possibly take more than half an hour or so a day."

The correct response to that would have been, "My ass." Hell, it would take me that long to get the microfilm machine loaded up. And am I supposed to go through every year's papers since we started publishing and find just the right tidbit every day?

I did inquire about that last part, and the publisher said he was sure I'd find something by perusing "only three or four years. Just use different years each time."

The length, I was told, was to be about three hundred words.

Stine must have noticed that I was on the verge of pulling out what scant hair I still have.

"Willie," he said, completely comfortable with the familiarity of first names now, "times have changed. We have to work smarter, not harder."

He actually said that. I thought that pearl of wisdom went out of happy horseshit management vernacular ten years ago.

"What about my days off?" I asked.

No problem, B.S. said.

"I'm sure you will be able to find time to squeeze in a couple of them on some days. There's always slow time on the night police beat."

Yeah, there is. And there are nights when the work isn't done until well after the last deadline, because those pesky criminals don't seem to have a deadline. I might be putting something on our website at two thirty in the morning, waking up Cindy with my big, cold feet sometime after three.

There was no way out of it, not without making our shiny new publisher think ol' Willie can't do the job anymore. I could only hope that something would happen to let this cup pass from me.

So the first day-in-history piece came out yesterday. Sarah Goodnight gave me the good news that, for some time, we have been able to peruse our archives digitally.

"You were going to do it all with microfilm?" she asked.

"I thought microfilm was a great technological advance," I said.

"Dinosaur," she replied.

I found a January 1 story from the 1920s in which a man accidentally shot his neighbor's dog while celebrating the New Year in a way of which the NRA would have approved. The one today, from the late fifties, was about a guy out in Henrico who was building his own bomb shelter. He was stocking it with, among other things, a one-year supply of pork and beans. Some things are worse than nuclear attacks, I'm thinking.

Between researching and writing, I spent about an hour and a half on each of those gems. Mercifully, the crime beat has been pretty quiet so far. This has cut into my solitaire playing though.

My primary editor, Sally Velez, said she thought I had a real future in writing about the past.

Sally did get me one bit of dispensation: This crap won't carry my byline.

—⁓—

FOR TOMORROW'S epic, I'm writing about a blizzard we had in the late forties in which the roof of a well-known restaurant collapsed under all the snow. If this gets any more exciting, the doctor will have to up my blood-pressure medication.

My thoughts, when I have time to think, go to Artie Lee. Maybe it's nosing through all these old files.

I'm hoping that a trip to Evergreen tomorrow will loosen Peggy's lips a little. Despite what my dear old mom says about hardly knowing my late father, Philomena told me they loved each other.

Something doesn't jibe here.

After I've turned in my third in what will be, unless I can find a way around it, a 365-day-a-year series, I ask Sally if could write something, if there's anything to write, about the dad I never knew. Maybe something down the road for Father's Day. I give her a little background.

She shrugs.

"What the hell. It's got to be better than that day-in-history crap. But when are you going to find time?"

I tell her that I plan to work smarter, not harder.

CHAPTER FOUR

Wednesday

Walter McGinnis's Prius is parked in front of my mother's house on Laurel Street.

Inside, I am greeted by my daughter and grandson, the lights, along with Cindy, of my otherwise dim life. Andi moved out of Peggy's place last year, mostly to appease the child-welfare people who frowned on her raising William in a house that, while suffused with love, also reeked of marijuana. She and William now share quarters with Walter over in the Fan, on Floyd Avenue. He seems to be taking good care of them. Andi and Walter haven't married, not yet at least, but that doesn't make Andi an outlier in the Black family.

"Is it better to not marry at all," Andi asked me recently, referring to her grandmother, "or just keep on doing it, like you, until you get it right?"

The clear message was that, with four nuptials on my rap sheet, I am not in a position to look askance on others' living arrangements. Touché.

Andi and Peggy are sitting on the couch, talking. William is being entertained by Awesome Dude. Awesome, whose emotional age is about four, is an appropriate playmate.

"I had a vacation day coming," Andi explains, "so William and I are paying a visit."

Andi seems to be bonding with social work, mostly with the homeless, even though another branch of that amorphous profession threatened to take her son away from her not long ago. She makes enough to pay for day care. Or, rather, she and Walter do. He's an accountant, and I think they earn more than either social workers or night cops reporters.

"Awesome is showing me how to play poker," my grandson says, trying to conceal the five cards he holds in his tiny hands. "We're playing for matches."

Could be worse. He could be showing William how to roll his own.

"He's a natural," Awesome says. Great.

"I told 'em their timing was bad," Peggy says. "Or maybe we could put off going to that damn graveyard."

Andi looks over at me.

"So you all are going to some cemetery where, what, my grandfather is buried? I didn't even know I had a grandfather. I mean . . . you know what I mean."

Yeah, neither Peggy nor I ever talked much about the ungainly family tree with Andi. Maybe my mom's not the only one in the Black family who wanted the past to be past.

"What was his name? Artie Lee? Why didn't you ever tell me about him? I don't even think I knew how he died."

I'm sure I told her that much, at some point, but nobody below a certain age cares a hell of a lot about genealogy.

"I don't know much about him," I tell Andi. "I'm just trying to keep a promise. There's nobody else to keep his grave clean."

"That's sad," she says. "I mean, that nobody cares enough to do that. It's kind of like he never existed."

I tell her that just about everybody gets forgotten eventually, even those folks in their fancy stone condos next door to Oregon Hill in Hollywood Cemetery. Even the two United States presidents buried there don't get much attention these days, I'm thinking.

It does kind of sting though. He was my damn father, no matter how absent he might have been. Maybe if he'd lived, we would have played catch or gone fishing or some such shit. And how can I blame him? I mean, death is a pretty good excuse for desertion.

I tell Peggy that we should go soon. Andi and William are invited to join us. Andi says she would love to, but she and my grandson are supposed to have a play date with another young mom and her two daughters.

"They're just crazy about William," Andi says.

And what woman wouldn't be, with his excellent chick-magnet genes?

—⁓—

AWESOME DUDE wants to come along, having nothing better to do. Awesome never has anything better to do.

"Dude," he says as he gets comfortable in the back seat, "it smells like cigarettes in here."

You get used to it, I tell him.

"Man," he says, "I'm glad I never picked up that habit."

We take the Downtown Expressway to I-64 East. The Nine Mile Road exit doesn't lead to the posh side of town. We're not far from where I have spent many evenings learning the particulars of various dirt naps so I could pass them on to our breathless readers.

Just beyond a house famous for being one of Robert E. Lee's umpteen headquarters in the Waw of Nawthen Aggression, I turn right.

Peggy sighs.

"Do we really have to do this crap? And if you needed me to come, why do you already know the way?"

I'm pretty sure I can find the cemetery, I tell her. I'm just not sure I can find Artie Lee.

"I hope I can," she says.

The road we take crosses over the interstate we recently exited. We follow a sign and turn onto a road that's about a lane and a half wide. There are tombstones along the side of it, many of them half-hidden in the underbrush. The cemetery seems to be bounded by some kind of landfill.

"This ain't it," Peggy says as she looks around. "Keep going."

Soon, we come to a pair of white posts with "Evergreen Cemetery" written on them, and we're there.

Straight ahead of us is a cleared space, a circle probably a couple of hundred yards across, where people seem to still be planting their loved ones. I see flowers and American flags on some of the flat stones.

Off to the right, though, is our destination. It must have been a nice place for a graveyard at one time. I can tell that it sits on a hill from which the view would be impressive, if there were a view.

The problem is the trees. Full-grown trees, which probably weren't even sprouts when this place opened in 1891, have taken over, surrounded by a thick tangle of underbrush. And it's worse than that. Evergreen truly is evergreen these days, but not in a good way. Ivy has covered all those now-grown trees and apparently choked the life out of them. Under a blanket of green is a dead forest waiting for the next hurricane to level it.

Peggy, who knows more than she's been letting on, has me turn right on a little rut path that leads back into a thicket from which more tombstones stick out. Many of them are leaning like little drunken ghosts. More than a few are lying on the ground.

It strikes me that I'm looking at death times two. The deceased are now in a cemetery that has itself passed on.

There are a few places where the underbrush has been cut back, but mostly it's a neglected necropolis.

Peggy directs me to take another turn, a left this time, past more ruined tombstones. And then we're at a place where the road stops and another path leads off to the left, back from where we came.

"There's Maggie Walker," Peggy says. "We're close."

I stop the car beside the marker commemorating the most famous person in Evergreen. Her grave and the area around it are clean, but the underbrush and neglect are on all sides, nipping at Maggie's heels. My mother leads us to a nearly invisible path, and we stumble downhill, tripping over fallen limbs and catching our pants legs in briers.

Two beer cans adorn a stone on my left. As I look around, the graves seem endless, leading down the hill to places that look like they haven't been touched in decades.

"There must be hundreds of these things," I offer.

"Thousands," Peggy says.

Finally, maybe one hundred feet off the rut road, Peggy stops and points.

"Over there."

At first I don't see it. There are a couple of family plots and a big-ass mausoleum farther down the hill that looks like it's been vandalized to a fare-thee-well. Many of the plots are marked off by rusted metal, family members united in death.

Artie Lee's grave, though, sits by itself.

The flat stone is maybe a foot high and eighteen inches wide, with just his name on the top. And it isn't Arthur something Lee. Just Artie Lee. The line underneath reads: Jan. 21, 1938–June 6, 1961.

Peggy kneels in front of the grave and brushes off dirt and debris. She removes the long-dead Christmas flowers and manages to pull up a greenbrier that has wrapped itself around the stone.

"Looks like somebody's tried to keep it clean."

"Philomena."

My mother looks up at me.

"She's a good woman."

I agree and note that it won't be that hard to maintain.

"You're goin' to have to come out here every month," Peggy says. "Them weeds grow fast. They can get the best of you."

I can see that she's right. There are some other Lees buried in the general vicinity of Artie's grave, their stones almost hidden. I assume that many of them share my DNA. I never promised Philomena that I'd look out for the whole damn family, but maybe I can keep the underbrush from completely taking over.

Awesome looks a little shaky.

"I don't like this place," he says.

I have to admit I'm not crazy about it either. Maybe on a warm spring day, it'd be OK. Now, though, with the wind moaning a dirge through the pines and the January chill settling into my damn bones, it isn't hard to see why the place isn't exactly a tourist attraction.

We're standing there, wondering if we've visited my late father's grave long enough, when we see another car approaching.

I recognize it. I did tell Richard we might come out here this morning, but I didn't really expect him to join us.

He makes his way downhill.

"I thought I'd see if I could still find it," he says after being introduced to Awesome and giving Peggy a hug. "Momma usually came out here by herself. Tell you the truth, I was glad to let her."

Richard Slade wasn't even born when my late father died, so I doubt that he can tell me much more about Artie Lee than I know already. Still, I have to ask.

"What was he like? I mean, did they ever talk about him or anything?"

Richard doesn't answer for a few seconds.

"Aw," he says at last, "you know, they used to tell stories. He didn't take any shit, excuse my language, he didn't take no stuff off of nobody, that's what they used to say about him."

He acts as if he wants to say more, but then he says, "I better shut up. I don't want to speak ill . . ."

"Of the dead" is the obvious conclusion to that sentence, but Richard Slade seems to want to move on to other topics. I can feel Peggy getting a little antsy.

We talk a little about Philomena, to whose side Richard will be returning shortly. We talk about Andi and William and the fact that it's supposed to snow tomorrow. We don't talk any more about Artie Lee.

I walk Richard back to his car. Peggy and Awesome linger to light up a joint. I hope they don't set the woods on fire, although a burn-off couldn't hurt this place.

I thank Richard for coming. He thanks me for assuming the mantle of grave-tender.

"It means a lot to her. She'll be happy not to have to worry about that."

It doesn't look as if Philomena is going to have to worry much about anything much longer, from what the doctors are telling Richard.

"I'm sorry," is all I can think to say.

"Oh, she's ready," Richard says. "She's right with the Lord. Don't know if I'm as sold on all that as she is, but if it sustains her, I say 'Praise Jesus.'

"But I'm goin' to miss her."

As he gets into the car, he looks up.

"Go see Arthur Meeks," he says. "He can tell you some stuff about Artie Lee. Him and Artie was tight, I understand."

Having been directed toward Mr. Meeks twice in three days, I suppose I'd be wise to do just that.

Peggy is back at the grave, tottering a little now, and not just from the uneven ground.

I help her back up to level footing, with Awesome following.

"So there's not anything you can tell me that you haven't told me already about my dear old dad?"

"It was all a long time ago," she says. "Why does everybody want to keep digging up the past?"

And then she starts talking. Maybe it's the dope. Whatever. I'll take information wherever I can find it. Maybe I ought to start getting my interview subjects stoned before I ask the tough questions.

"I met him at a dance," Peggy says.

I stop and listen.

The dance was at a club that hasn't existed for a long time. Everybody there was white except the band. She had come with two girlfriends, one of whom had a car and a driver's license. They were all juniors in high school.

"Artie played the saxophone. Tenor sax. I hadn't ever seen anybody play music like that, not in person. It was like the music was inside him, like him and it were the same thing

"I liked Jerry Lee Lewis and all that lively stuff. But I'd never heard anything like Artie Lee and that saxophone."

When the band took a break, she went to the bathroom and then stepped outside for a smoke.

"You smoked? Tobacco, I mean."

"That was a long time ago. They didn't know it would kill you back then."

I clear my throat. She gives me a piercing look.

"Don't interrupt," she says.

Artie Lee was there, leaning against the side of the cinder-block building.

"He looked at me, and I looked at him. And then he came over and started talking to me. There weren't that many people around to give us the fish-eye about him being black and me being white. Maybe they gave him a pass because he was in the band. I don't know.

"But something clicked."

Peggy says they talked for maybe five minutes, and she felt like she had found somebody special. She doesn't say "soul mate," but I get her drift.

"He was so handsome. He had this pale brown skin, not much more than a good suntan, and a sharp face, like his cheekbones and chin had been chiseled. But I think I'd have been attracted to him even if he'd been ugly. And when he smiled, and I'd come to find out he didn't do that very much, it lit up the room.

"We just hit it off."

Just when she's whetted my appetite, Peggy says we need to get back. Awesome, who's been keeping his distance while we talk, comes over and seconds that motion. It kind of breaks the spell.

"But what kind of man was he? What happened after that?"

Tell me something, dammit.

Peggy shrugs as she walks ahead of me toward the car.

"We sneaked around, which was all we could do. I had you about the time I was supposed to graduate from high school. Don't that tell you what you need to know?

"Now can you please get us the hell out of here? This place gives me the creeps."

—⁂—

I TREAT her and Awesome to lunch at the Robin Inn, where Peggy has ordered the same damn thing as long as I can remember: small pizza with Italian sausage. She can't weigh one hundred pounds, but she eats like a horse, probably enhanced by her cannabis appetizer. She finishes the whole pie. Awesome, not used to dining in restaurants, seems almost as uneasy as he was at the cemetery. That doesn't stop him from finishing off a small pepperoni pizza though.

I drop them off and head home. Butterball must be fed. The cat seems to get bigger every time I look at her. Cindy says she's just big boned.

I saved a few pieces of chicken liver from my own entrée and now slip them into the cat's canned food. The look the animal gives me when she tastes it is as close to gratitude as Butterball ever comes.

"Don't get used to it," is my advice on the way out.

By the time I check in at the word factory, things are in high gear, or at least as high as we get in our layoff-riddled, four-cylinder newsroom.

We—and by "we," I mean the people who wear suits and make the kind of decisions that have brought us to our current state—have decided that what modern journalism needs is more meteorology. Forget politics. Forget the hard-pressed schools and the opioid crisis. What we must give our readers, it has been decreed, is more weather news.

OK, I see where they're coming from. The local news on any of our Richmond TV stations is one extended weather forecast with news sprinkled in. First they tell you how hot or cold it got today, teasing you that more is coming. ("Could snow be in the forecast?") Then they throw some real news at you. Then they tell you what the weather might be like tomorrow. Then it's more non-meteorological stuff, but by now we're down to the obligatory cute pet story and the forty-five seconds they give sports. Finally, you get the payoff: what the weather will be like for the next five days. After all that wait, they're often wrong, but weather forecasters don't seem to run corrections.

Some brainiac on the suit floor has deduced that if it's good enough for TV, it's good enough for us.

And, with actual snow seemingly inevitable for tomorrow, we are fired up.

Benson Stine is actually in the newsroom, a place he hardly ever frequents. He wants hourly reports. He wants somebody out there all night, in what could be close to zero-degree weather, so we can post something online. He wants reports on panicky mobs stripping the shelves of milk, beer, and diapers. The guy they've hired solely to cover weather looks like he's about to have an orgasm right in the newsroom. It's his moment to shine.

Our publisher spies me before I can duck into the coffee-break room.

"Ah, Willie," he says. "Let's try to find a good weather story for the look-back. I'm sure we must have had a big snow on January 4 at some time in our history."

No doubt. Now all I have to do is find it.

What the hell. It's too damn cold to shoot anybody. Night cops should be quiet. Unless one of the space heaters the city has provided for our public-housing residents after their heating system died burns one of the buildings down, I've got time to kill.

It looks like I'm stuck with Today in Richmond History for some time to come. Early reports indicate that the same people who are crazy for more weather news get a hard-on reading about the past too. In Richmond, where the past is never past, I guess that makes sense. I wish it didn't, because I'm thinking this gig is going to get pretty damn old before the forsythias bloom.

"Be thankful," Sally Velez says. "The look-backs might save your job."

As I peruse the digital files looking for a January 4 blizzard worthy of B3, it occurs to me that I'm in no position to look askance at the weather guy. At least he gets a breaking story now and then.

I get lucky and find an acceptable snowstorm in about forty-five minutes. I give our readers a breathless account of it in another thirty or so.

Not that I'd admit it to Sally or anyone else. Pretending to drag this epistle out for another couple of hours gives me time to check on something else in the archives:

The death of Artie Lee.

CHAPTER FIVE

Thursday

The weather dude had it right this time. We woke up this morning to enough snow to keep us entertained without it being a major pain in the ass. We watched it fall onto Monroe Park, which we can see over the top of the damn barricades the city has installed while the park gets a makeover.

Hell, I didn't think it needed a makeover, but apparently there were too many trees there. I worry that the homeless won't have enough shade when the renovation is done.

The snow is pretty though. And, since even a cloudy day is reason enough to close all the schools around Richmond, Cindy has the day off, which gives us a morning to snuggle and watch it come down. I wish our publisher was as concerned for our safety as the school superintendents are for the kiddies' well-being.

We didn't get a paper this morning. I know we put one out last night, because I was there until the bitter end. And we live only ten blocks from the newsroom. I know the printing plant is way out in the boondocks, but it doesn't look that slick outside, from what I can see of Franklin Street.

The last time it snowed enough to matter, I was holding forth on our inability to get a paper in my mitts at the Prestwould in a timely fashion. Handley Pace in design, who has more of a feel for modern technology than yours truly (and who doesn't?), told me he was pretty sure why we aren't keeping up with even the damn post office in the category of prompt delivery.

"It's the website," he explained.

At some point, he said, somebody on high figured that we could avoid the hassle and overtime and occasional wreck involved in home delivery on snowy days by telling people to just read it online.

Some people, I told Hanley, aren't online. And other people really enjoy the tactile element of working their way through the morning paper as they sit by the fire drinking their morning coffee. The iPad Mini Cindy gave me for Christmas doesn't give me the same warm, fuzzy feeling.

So, not only does technology somehow make our deadlines earlier every time, it also gives the money guys an excuse to not deliver the goods.

Missing paper notwithstanding, it is not a bad day to sit here by our gas-log fireplace and enjoy nature's show.

"You know," Cindy says, "those windows in the bedroom have a pretty good view of the park too."

Later, lazing in the sheets, she asks me what else I've been able to find out about my father. I told her last night that I'd had time to do a little investigating.

"So, did you find anything?"

"Maybe."

—⁓—

WHAT I found raised more questions than it answered, as is often the case.

The key is knowing when to stop digging and start writing. We had a guy who worked here until about ten years ago who was assigned to do a story on the disparity in sentencing in our fair commonwealth between black and white criminals. Anybody with eyes and ears knew there was a big-ass gap there. We just wanted to know how bad it was.

The reporter, though, got his teeth into it and, like a pit bull with lockjaw, just couldn't let go. A year later, he still hadn't published, and one of the conference rooms was half-full of boxes of notes. He always needed just one more factoid, just had to talk to one more judge or ex-con or prisoner advocate.

In the end, with a gun to his head, he did finally finish the series, but it was so long and tedious that they should have made it required reading for the convicted, as part of their punishment. I think it won second place in investigative reporting in the state press contest. The guy left to take a job, God help us, teaching journalism.

This isn't a damn newspaper series though. This is a man's life. My father's life. And although I might someday write what I find, I need to know a hell of a lot more than I do now, and I'm not likely to stop digging until I hit bottom.

Last night, while I was still pretending to search for that elusive bygone blizzard, I went back to June of 1961.

If the gravestone was correct, Artie Lee died on the sixth of June, the anniversary of D-Day. It was, I learned, a Tuesday. So I looked at the next day's editions. Nothing there.

I went to Thursday, and there it was, on the second page of the local section:

"Negro man killed/ in Charles City crash"

The story was eight paragraphs long. My father was the lone occupant of the car, the story said. The wreck happened about nine P.M. The car hit a tree, and that was it for Artie Lee, who, our rag reported, died at the scene.

The last paragraph:

"A witness who was walking along Route 5 claimed he saw two other men standing alongside Lee's car, stopped on the highway, but he couldn't identify them. Police are investigating."

I looked at papers for the next two weeks, searching for some further information. Whatever investigating the police did apparently did not yield anything worthy of print. Maybe my paper lost interest in a black man's death. Maybe, it being 1961, the cops did too.

I read the paid obituary, which didn't tell me much. The pallbearers were all names I didn't know, except for one: Arthur Meeks. No mention, of course, of Peggy or his half-breed son over in Oregon Hill.

Artie Lee, I realized, would have been eighty years old in a little more than two weeks. Maybe, had he lived, he and Peggy would have married in better times, making me an honest boy. Maybe I'd have been their teenage ring bearer. Maybe, maybe, maybe.

Even as I was digesting the fuzzy details of Artie Lee's demise, I was already writing the lede in my mind for a January 21 tearjerker:

"The father I never knew would have turned eighty today."

If I could stop being a cynical bastard who sometimes puts a good story ahead of his humanity, I would. It's a curse.

Now I know more than I knew before last night, but a hell of a lot less than I want to.

—〜〜—

"So, somebody thought he saw somebody else there, but you can't find anything else in the paper?" Cindy asks as she sits up and stretches.

"Maybe there was something else, later. I don't know."

"But wouldn't your mother know?"

Yeah, she ought to, I'm thinking.

I get out of bed and open the window enough to enjoy my first smoke of the day without befouling the place and pissing off Kate, my landlady and ex-wife. I make the call.

Peggy answers on the fifth ring, just as her voice mail kicks in. I tell her to hang up and let me call back.

I inform her of the newspaper article I read last night.

I hear her curse.

"You're not going to give it up, are you? Can't you just keep the beer cans off his grave and let it go at that?"

I probably sound a tad pissed off as I note that it would seem that she might have been slightly interested in the fact that the man with whom she had a son had died under what might be considered mysterious circumstances.

"You don't know," she says, yelling into the phone. I can hear Awesome Dude in the background, trying to calm her down. "You wasn't there."

"Actually, I was, remember? I was, what, fifteen months old, not old enough yet to know that I didn't have a daddy."

There is a silence on the other end of the line. I wonder if Peggy has hung up.

Finally, she speaks.

"They didn't say anything to me."

"Who?"

"The police. They might of talked to his folks, but we weren't married or nothing, so they kind of shut me out."

I ask her if she tried to find out anything from the police.

"Yeah," she says after a pause. "I talked to the police. I asked a cop I knew, Eddie Shaw, he grew up right down the street, a few years ahead of me in school. You know what he said?"

I wait.

"He said this was what I got for screwing around with niggers, and that the police had better things to do than take some pickaninny kid's word about seeing somebody else there.

"He said Artie Lee ran off the road and hit a tree. End of story."

I can hear her sigh.

"Eddie was a mean bastard, probably still is. I wanted to claw his eyes out, but I didn't. He was the law, and he wasn't above doing anything. He might have even got social services to take you away from me. So I just shut up and took it."

I apologize for digging up that kind of memory.

"Aw," she says, calmer now, "you got a right. He was your daddy, no matter what.

"You know," she continues when I think she's said all she's going to say, "that old son of a bitch still has a house here, but I think he's moved somewhere on South Side. He must be over eighty years old now. Came from a long line of sons of bitches. He was uncle to that Shiflett boy, the one that died in the fire."

Good lord. The guy she's talking about, whom I don't remember, is David Shiflett Junior's uncle. Shiflett was a detective with Richmond's finest until he was bound, gagged, and burned to death by the grief-crazed father of the girl Shiflett killed. I know because I watched it happen from fifteen feet away.

Made a hell of story, after Peggy's boyfriend, the much-lamented Les Hacker, arrived like the cavalry and saved my ass.

But, because we don't like to dwell on unpleasantness here in the Holy City, "died in the fire" sums it up rather nicely.

"Willie," my mother says, "put it behind you. I have."

Not much chance of that.

—m—

THE PAPER is a 24/7/365 deal, even if we can't be bothered to deliver the damn thing the next morning.

So I'm at work not much after two thirty. There hasn't been that much snow, but it's cold as a bitch, and those brick sidewalk stretches between the Prestwould and the office are a skating rink. I fall on my ass halfway there. Thank God for strong bones. A man with no fixed address comes out of nowhere, helps me up and asks me if I can spare a buck. I give him a five. If he's out and about today, he needs it more than I do.

I expect a quiet day. Maybe I can get a few editions ahead on Today in Richmond History. Newsroom wiseasses already are calling it the Morgue Report, the ones old enough to remember what a newspaper morgue is.

Instead, I find the newsroom is a drama pit. Word has gotten out, as it always does, that we soon won't have a features department. We've been relying more and more on freelancers and the wire services for feature stories, reviews, and other crap that used to be lumped together in less-enlightened times in the "women's section."

Now, though, it's official. The news is a little surprising, even at a place where the next round of layoffs is always just around the corner. After all, we recently invested a lot of puffery into promoting a "new and improved" culture section on Wednesdays that was to be just chock-full of word candy for the aesthetic crowd. We even hired a reporter just to dive headfirst into the artsy-fartsy world. Joke's on him, I guess.

The new, "improved" culture section, from what our informed sources are telling us, will consist largely of recipes, most of them not involving meat.

But the joke's also on a bunch of mostly good folks who have been here for a while. Goodbye, decent salary. Hello, Obamacare.

"There used to be like thirty-six people in that department," Sally Velez says as we watch well-wishers offer useless platitudes to people who are watched closely by human resources personnel as they are allowed to clean out their desks and get the hell out of the building. We're not much on gold watches around here these days. Our corporate masters at MediaWorld are more into offering two months' severance pay and their best wishes. The publisher and his suit-mates are always absent at times like this. They're probably taking a snow day.

"We used to have a guy who just covered local theater, a guy who did classical music. A woman who just covered television," Sally says.

She ought to know. She was the features editor in one of her many incarnations here.

We used to have a lot of stuff, I remind her.

"And now we've got the goddamn weather," she says.

"Don't forget the Morgue Report," I remind her.

We look at each other. I am sure she's feeling what I'm feeling: survivor guilt, also known as "Thank God it wasn't me this time."

So being chained to Today in Richmond History is far from the worst fate around here. I feel guilty for bitching. Not guilty enough to stop though. As the main architect of three divorces, I can live with guilt.

The woman who was, a far as we can see, the last features editor this rag will ever have comes over to Sally and hands her a couple of plaques. We look closely and see that they're both national awards given to feature sections deemed to be among the top ten in the nation. Both of them were given out in the past five years.

Journalists give themselves too many awards. The national ones, though, are pretty meaningful. Or should be.

"Here," the editor says, "when you get a chance, could you take these to our publisher? Ask him to see if he can shove them up his fat ass."

Sally gives her a hug and promises that she'll leave them on his desk, with the proper though anonymous instructions.

And then those of us who still have jobs get back to work.

—∽—

AT LEAST we have early deadlines, although probably not early enough to get papers to all our readers tomorrow morning.

I am able to vacate the premises a little after nine. I catch the Number 16 bus back to the Prestwould, but I don't go inside, much as I want to.

I've already called police headquarters and found out that the eminent Larry Doby Jones took a sick day today. Can't blame him, but there's something I really need to talk with our chief about.

Maybe it's better if I pay a home visit to L.D., for this one anyhow.

So I spend ten minutes scraping snow off my super-annuated Honda, call Cindy up on the sixth floor to tell her I'll be home in an hour or so, and head for the North Side.

I've been to the chief's house a couple of times, but things have been a bit strained between us the last few years. L.D.'s goals and mine often don't mesh. Mainly, I want to print the news and the chief wants to suppress it. It has cast a pall on my relationship with my old pickup basketball partner.

He lives over by Virginia Union University, in a neighborhood that was started by African Americans who somehow found a way to buy nice homes in the first half of the twentieth century.

Belinda answers the door. She and L.D. have been married longer than I have, pretty amazing consider-ing that my matrimonial record spans four brides.

She seems delighted to see me. Somehow, the chief's distaste for me hasn't infected his better half. Either that, or she just has better manners.

After giving me a hug and wondering why I don't come around more often, she points me to L.D.'s man cave in the basement, which I invade near the end of the first half of a college basketball game of no great importance.

He's in one of those recliners that returns you to the full upright position automatically but rather slowly. Maybe that's why the chief doesn't rise to greet me. At least he doesn't tell me to get the fuck out. I'm hoping for a kinder, gentler L.D. Jones than the one with whom I usually interact.

"What you want?" he inquires.

"I want to know something about a single-car fatality," I tell him.

His look tells me that his estimation of my intelligence, already at sea level, is now under water.

"You come up here on a night like this to ask me about a damn wreck? Must be a slow news day."

"Yeah, but it happened a while back."

"When?"

"June 6, 1961."

He is intrigued enough to manipulate the chair so that his feet are eventually on the ground.

"Nineteen sixty-one? You want to know about some shit that happened fifty-seven years ago?"

"Well, it's kind of personal."

So I tell the chief about my father and Philomena Slade and Evergreen, eventually getting to the part where I found that article in the newspaper.

"Yeah," he says, "I know something about Evergreen. I think I have a couple of great uncles buried over there, but damned if I could find their graves. And I sure as hell remember Philomena Slade."

He would. The Slade case, in which Richard Slade turned out to be innocent of a crime for which L.D. and his minions were convinced he was guilty, was part of why the chief and I don't exchange Christmas cards these days.

He tells me that anything from that far back would not be in anybody's files anymore.

"So there's no way to find out whatever happened to Artie Lee?"

He stands up, with great effort. I don't think the chief has been going to the gym much lately.

"Willie," he says, "are you new around here? Did you just fall off the turnip truck? He was a black man. It was back in the day. I would hazard a guess that not a hell of a lot of effort went into finding those two men, if there were two other men."

Yeah, he's probably right.

"I know he was your daddy and all, but whatever happened to him happened. Nobody was going to work overtime to tie that one up."

He says he'll check around though.

I tell him I appreciate that. We shake hands, something we haven't done in years.

As I start to leave, he says, "But you didn't even know where he was buried, until the Slade woman told you?"

I stop, turn, and tell him I've been asked that a lot lately.

"I was fifteen months old, L.D., last time they tell me I saw him. He and my mom never married, couldn't have if they'd wanted to. He wasn't exactly on my radar."

The chief is almost apologetic when he says he understands.

"I was playing ball one day, over at the park, must have been fourteen years old. This old guy, looked like a bum, he calls me over, knows my name. I didn't come at first, because I didn't know him from Adam.

"Finally, I walk over, ask him what the hell he wants.

"And he says, 'Don't you know me, boy? Don't you know your daddy?'

"I thought he was full of crap and told him so. He was kind of small and beat down. I think I could've taken him in a fight. But he just looked at me, and then he turned and walked off."

L.D. says he went home right after that and asked his mother about it.

"She just looked at me and said I didn't have a daddy, that if I had a daddy, he'd have shown his ass up before now so she didn't have to work two jobs. But she said his name, said he'd split a long time ago. I had asked her about it before, and that was the first time she ever even acknowledged his name.

"I never saw the man again, don't know where he came from that day or why he came, but I never looked for him. I sure as hell don't know where he's buried."

I give the chief a "fair enough" nod.

"At least," he says to my back, "yours didn't choose to leave you."

CHAPTER SIX

Friday

The radiator pipes are playing the Anvil Chorus, staving off the cold. What snow we had yesterday looks like it'll stick around for a while. The people I see on the sidewalk below are trying to walk carefully and fast at the same time.

Cindy gets another day off today. We don't spend enough money on snow and ice treatment down here to have everything cleared off in a timely fashion. People who come to work at the paper from points north seem to think this makes Richmond incredibly provincial.

We had a reporter a few years back who moved here from Buffalo. He couldn't stop talking about how retarded we were when it came to snow.

"You can't drive in it," I heard him say one day when four inches of snow had turned Franklin Street into a parking lot. "You can't afford to remove it. You act like it's Armageddon every time a few flakes fall."

Enos Jackson, who's now on what's left of the copy desk and never leaves Richmond except to go to a cottage on Assateague two weeks every summer, had heard the routine a couple of times that day. He finally enlightened our immigrant.

"If I lived in fucking Buffalo," Enos explained, "I'd be able to drive in snow, because I'd have to do it eight damn months a year. Practice makes perfect. If I lived in Buffalo, I'd pay the taxes to make sure the roads were clear of that hundred inches of snow you get, because otherwise, it'd be like the Donner party. We'd have to eat the kids. But that's all kind of moot, because if I lived in Buffalo, I would have blown my fucking brains out a long time ago."

Actually, the streets I see look to be in pretty good shape. Maybe the city hasn't depleted its road-salt budget yet.

Cindy is enjoying her second cup of coffee. She's sitting by the window, watching the hawk watching the squirrels in the park as it tries to figure out which one to have for breakfast.

I tell her that I'm going out.

"In this crap? Where?"

"To find Arthur Meeks."

"Who?"

I explain that Mr. Meeks has been recommended to me twice in the past few days as a possible source of information about Artie Lee.

"Willie," she says, "why is this so important? I mean, it's commendable that you're going to look after the grave, but there isn't much you can find out that you don't know already, is there?"

I tell her that I don't know, but that I intend to find out.

"Do you even know where he lives?"

I'm pretty sure I do. If the Google Map hasn't steered me wrong, I'll actually be on the same Nine Mile Road I was on two days ago, just farther down.

Cindy says she'll be very happy to sit by the fire with Butterball in lieu of a road trip. She cautions me to be careful. Butterball doesn't seem to care much one way or the other.

The map works fine. Most of our friends seem to prefer having the nice lady on the dashboard tell them where to go, but it still pleases me more to have a map, even if it's one printed off a computer, and even if I have to stop twice on the way to refresh my memory.

It would have been smarter to call ahead. I tried, but nobody answered the phone at the address I found for who seems to be the only Arthur Meeks living in the greater Richmond area. Hell, this could be Arthur Meeks Jr., or some other Arthur Meeks altogether.

I also could have waited for a more pleasant day, but after so many years of giving little or no thought to Artie Lee, I find myself to be a man on a mission.

The Meeks residence, near Sandston out by the airport, is what a generous person would call modest. It looks like fifties vintage, complete with aluminum siding. There can't be more than twenty feet between the house and the ones on either side.

The doorbell doesn't seem to be working. I knock, wait, then knock again.

Finally, I hear someone walking—or shuffling, to be more precise—in the direction of the front door.

The door cracks open slightly.

"What is it?" the figure I can barely make out asks, not kindly.

I explain quickly, before he shuts me out in the cold again, that I am Artie Lee's son and am looking for someone who knew him.

"Artie Lee? Artie Lee? What the hell you talking about, Artie Lee?"

He acts like he doesn't know who I'm talking about. Then, his memory kicks in.

"Oh, Artie Lee. Yeah."

But I'm still not in the door. Meeks scratches his nuts and frowns.

"Artie Lee didn't have no son."

I explain that he did indeed have a son, and that I'm him. I tell him about Artie and Peggy.

"Can I come in, sir?" I ask him. "I'm freezing my butt off out here."

He does open the door wider then.

I get my first good look at him. I figure he's about eighty, like my father would be had he lived. He probably was a lot taller at one point, but I swear to God he can't be more than five two, and he probably wouldn't crack one hundred on the scales. And he's using a cane.

I drop Philomena Slade's name. Everybody seems to know Philomena, so it puts me at least marginally in Arthur Meeks's good graces.

"Yeah, I heard she wasn't doing so good," he says. "Well, tell her I'm praying for her."

He offers me a glass of water. I accept just to make the conversation last a little longer, then regret it when I realize I've made a shrunken old man limp over to the kitchen to draw me a glass of eau de Sandston. There's a TV sitting ten feet from Meeks's chair, maybe the last analog television in the world. It's sitting atop another set that must have died some time ago.

When he gets back, I tell him about what I found in that 1961 newspaper about how Artie Lee died.

"The paper said a boy saw it and said he saw two other men standing by the car, but there wasn't anything else about it that I could find. I was hoping you could tell me something."

Meeks sits back in his chair. He pulls a blanket over his legs. The room we're in has an oil heater sitting in one corner, and I'm guessing that's all he's got to heat the whole house. Even in here, it isn't enough.

"Artie Lee, he was a pistol," the old man says. "He was indeed. When he died, it hit us hard. He could play that music like nobody's business."

I ask him again if he knows anything about how my father died.

He goes off on a story about Artie and his band playing somewhere down in Farmville, and their station wagon broke down, and the local cops were threatening to throw them all in the jail. The story doesn't seem to have an end. It might not even have a middle.

When Meeks stops to catch his breath, I try to bring the conversation around again to Artie Lee's death.

He looks at me and shakes his head. He is silent for what seems like a full minute. My old reporter's strategy of dummying up to make the subject talk doesn't seem to be working.

Finally, he looks at me with his yellow, bloodshot eyes.

"They always said it was an accident," he says. "But, young man, sometimes an accident isn't no accident, you know what I mean."

I tell him I wish I did know what he meant, but he says he doesn't want to talk any more about Artie Lee.

"But you're his boy," he says, veering off topic again. "Well, I can see a little of him in you, although I'm betting you pass for white most of the time."

Not on purpose, I tell him.

"Well," the old man says, smiling and showing me a mouth about half full of teeth, "take what you can get."

Arthur Meeks says he and Artie Lee and another man, Arkie Bright, used to hang out together.

"We were the Triple-A boys," he says. "Artie, Arthur, and Arkie. Arkie played in the band, too, I think. Arkie's still around. Full name's Archangel. Maybe he could tell you something about your daddy."

When I ask him again what he means about accidents not being accidents, he says that was just an old man talking, that he "don't know nothing."

I ask him if he has any photos of Artie. He says he doesn't, but then he corrects himself.

"Just a minute," he says.

He comes back in more like ten minutes. He has an old photo album with him. Another five minutes yields the picture he was looking for.

"There we are," he says. "The Triple-A boys."

And there they are. They all look to be in their early or mid-twenties, all bright and shiny and full of hope. Meeks points to Artie Lee, standing in the middle with his arms around his friends.

"We was tight," he says.

I am briefly undone. It is the first time I have ever seen a photo of the man who was my father. If Peggy had one, she's never showed it to me.

He is, as I knew, light-skinned, much more pale than his two friends. I can tell that even in the black-and-white photograph. He's tall, at least compared with Arthur and Arkie, and he looks like he might weigh one hundred forty pounds with rocks in his pockets. He's either smiling or smirking. He looks like a man who was susceptible to mischief.

I ask Arthur Meeks if I can take a picture of the photo with my iPhone. He seems amazed that there is such a thing as a phone that takes pictures.

"I don't get out that much," he says. "My children live up around DC. They don't come down here much. I don't have much use for all that new stuff."

Me either, I assure him.

He urges me again to talk to Arkie Bright, who "lives somewhere in Blackwell, I think. Haven't seen him in years, but I think he's still above ground."

I thank him for his time.

On the way out, I realize that Arthur Meeks has managed to whet my curiosity even more, mostly by trying to tamp it down.

—⁓—

THE TRIP back to the Prestwould is only briefly delayed by an overturned truck in the right-hand lane of I-64.

The handful of residents who are socializing in the lobby seem stunned that I would go out "on a day like this." The ones who are there are mostly in their late seventies and eighties. I wonder how much longer before the idea of driving on ice will terrify me too. They can still party though. A couple of wine bottles and a half-gallon of bourbon sit on the counter over by where the guard sits at night.

Clara Westbrook, my favorite of the old crowd, is sporting a glass containing brown liquid. I ask her if there's anything I can get her, from a grocery store or elsewhere.

"Thank you, Willie," she says, "but I think I have enough bourbon and Scotch for at least three more days."

—⁓—

UPSTAIRS, A surprise awaits me.

"Look who's here," Cindy says.

Who's here are Abe Custalow and his mostly faithful companion, Stella Stellar. Abe looks about the same. Stella's hair is green this week. My old roomie has been living with Ms. Stellar, who's still trying to make her mark in the music world, since Abe's son died.

I think but don't say how ironic it is that Abe has lost his only known child and I'm chasing the ghost of my father. I see him from time to time in the building, but he hasn't been in the sixth-floor unit he, Cindy, and I shared for a while since he packed up his stuff and left.

Everybody seems nice and cozy. Looking at Abe, you'd think nothing had happened to blight our life-long friendship.

Abe's not even supposed to be in today. Being slave to his conscience, he came in anyhow, just to make sure the cold weather hadn't done violence to our heating system.

"And I thought I'd drop by. Haven't seen this place since . . ."

Yeah. Since then.

"Go on, you knucklehead," Stella lovingly encourages him.

Abe stands and asks if he can speak to me in private.

We go into the study, to which I retreat when there's a ball game on that conflicts with an old movie that Cindy wants to watch on the big TV in the living room. I sit in the chair by my computer, giving Custalow the one that's actually comfortable.

I ask him what's on his mind.

"Stella's got a gig," he says. "That half-ass band she's with has actually got somebody to do a CD, and they're going to be on the road for like two months."

I express my pleasure. Yeah, the Goldfish Crackers were pretty good, when I saw them, but I'm always running into some band that plays better music than a lot of what I hear on the radio, and most of them never make any money at it, other than doing parties and weddings and giving music lessons to kids.

"I think the drummer knew somebody in the business," Abe says. "Anyhow, they're hitting the road. Stella thinks this is her big chance."

I wait for it.

"So she says she can save money by letting her lease lapse. It runs out at the end of the month. Truth is, I think she believes they're headed for bigger things and might be looking at Richmond in the rearview mirror."

I can see where this is going.

"I was wondering . . ."

"We haven't sold the bed or the chairs. Rent's the same as it was before."

"Are you sure? I mean, do you want to talk it over with Cindy? I mean, you two probably want to have a little privacy."

I tell him that I'll talk to her, but I know what the answer will be. It's been kind of lonesome around here since Abe departed. Plus, the way he took off, it left me with some serious guilt. I'd do what I did again, if I had the chance. Saving Custalow at the expense of his damn train wreck of a son is not a dilemma I would wish to encounter again, but I did what I had to do.

"If it gets too crowded in here," I tell Abe, "we'll just tell you to get the fuck out."

I ask him if he's OK, an all-encompassing question that leaves the answer in his court.

He scratches his ear.

"It hurts," he says. "I won't deny that it does. I wish there was some way it could have worked out better.

"But you did what you thought you had to do. You wanted to save me. Again."

I tell him that he saved himself the first time. Sure, he was at a low point when I found him among the homeless in Monroe Park back then, but Abe Custalow would have found a way to get back on track. I am sure of that and tell him so.

We're guys. We don't do feelings worth a shit.

"Well," he says, "anyhow . . ."

"Room's ready when you are."

We hug. Don't tell anyone.

Back in the living room, I congratulate Stella on her upcoming big break.

"So," I ask, "are you still going by 'Goldfish Crackers,' now that you're hitting the big time?"

"Sure," she says, "why would we change a great name like that?"

Indeed.

Cindy already knows the score. She tells Abe how happy she is that he's coming back to live with us.

"Are you sure?" he asks her.

"Yeah, I'm sure. With Willie working five nights a week, I'm glad for the company."

She looks at me.

"Hope you don't take that the wrong way, sweetie."

No problem, I tell her, especially after I have the cameras set up in the living room and bedrooms.

Cindy winks at Stella.

"What happens in the Prestwould, stays in the Prestwould."

After Abe and Stella leave, I thank Cindy for being so considerate.

She asks me about my visit with Arthur Meeks.

"Sounds like he knows more than he's telling," she says when I've told her what I learned, or didn't.

I tell her that everybody seems to know more about Artie Lee than I do.

CHAPTER SEVEN

Saturday

Last night should have been a snoozer. With the thermometer sinking toward zero, who has the want-to to venture outside and kill somebody?

It turns out that four of our local felons were not about to let a little cold weather keep them from their appointed rounds.

One of them shot a teenager dead while the kid was sitting in his car over in Gilpin Court. No doubt there was some kind of misunderstanding. It's amazing how often people around here, given the choice of working out their differences or resorting to gunfire, just lock and load. The victim was seventeen years old. I'm betting the shooter will turn out to be on the low side of eighteen as well.

There's a program in the local school system, called Podium or Rostrum or Lectern or some such shit, that tries to teach young bloods to talk to each other instead of immediately firing away. Can't wait for that to show more results.

At least there wasn't a crowd. Two above zero served as a deterrent to the curious, so the boy who was lying dead, halfway out the driver's-side door, didn't have a bunch of younger kids gawking at his frosty corpse.

The other shooting, also resulting in death, took place in a little convenience store down off the Jeff Davis Highway. They haven't looked at the store's surveillance cameras yet, but a witness said three young punks came in. One of them had a gun. He pointed it at the guy behind the counter, who was the owner, an Indian immigrant with a wife and kids, and then he just shot him. Didn't even give him a chance to hand over whatever was in the register. Maybe the kid was nervous. Maybe it was his first holdup. All three of them turned and ran when they realized what they'd done. They didn't even bother to rob the damn place.

They'll catch them in no time flat, and all three probably will spend most or all of their adult lives in places that will make them far worse citizens than they were when they went in.

So what's the answer? Justice or mercy? Old Testament or New? Some judge or jury might deduce that justice for three punks who killed a man with a family to support, for no good reason, would be a long, slow, torturous death. And they might also opt to throw in a dollop of mercy and give the perps forty years each.

Andi tells me about the terrible things she's seen and stories she's heard as a social worker: kids basically raised by wolves, fending for themselves at an age when precious suburban youths are in pre-kindergarten, with two parents spending all their waking, nonwork hours ensuring that Junior and Missy have a chance to be all they can be at lacrosse or field hockey.

I sympathize. I haven't been there, but I've been halfway there as a mixed-race, single-parent kid in Oregon Hill.

Still, though, I saw that Indian man lying in his own guts. I saw his wife run past the police and throw herself on his body, every bit of hope drained out of her.

So if some judge says forty years, I can live with that. Mercy's a whole lot easier to dole out if your shoe soles aren't sticky with an innocent man's blood.

And then, adding to last night's drama, there were the overdoses. Most of the reporters here have learned how to spell opioids by now. A thirty-something mother on the North Side stopped breathing last night. She'd been to rehab twice. Obviously, it didn't take. And a truck driver from Mechanicsville is on life support. And that was just one day. Yeah, there's a lot bigger outcry among the general public than there was when crack was king, and a cynic would say that opioids get the paper's attention because suburban folks—you know, *real* people—are biting the dust. Whatever the reason, though, I'll be happy when this latest gift from hell wears out. I know, though, that something else will take its place. The urge to self-destruct and the entrepreneurial ingenuity of evil bastards will see to that.

—ɷ—

THIS MORNING, I make a visit to the hospital, where Richard Slade looks as if he hasn't slept in a week.

"She's hanging on," he tells me. The doctors aren't giving him much reason to hope.

"They wanted to know if she has a living will," he says. "Hell, she doesn't have any kind of will that I know of. They said they needed it, just in case. I suppose just in case she's, you know, not able to stay alive on her own."

I suggest that Richard might try to see if Philomena wants to make any kind of decision like that.

"Nah, man," he says. "We ain't goin' there. We ain't going to pull the damn plug until her soul drifts away. I'm afraid to leave here for fear they'll do something while I'm gone, just to free up the bed."

I tell him I don't think they'd do that. I do offer, though, to sit with his mother for an hour or so in order for him to grab breakfast or just a breath of air that doesn't smell like medicine and impending death.

He takes me up on the offer. Philomena's niece, Chanelle, has been spelling him some, he says, "but she's got a job, too, where they don't give you time off just because your auntie might be dying."

I ask him about his job. I know he's gotten on at Dupont.

"I got some vacation time," he says. "Here's where I ought to be."

Philomena seems to be sleeping. I don't wake her up, but maybe she's just resting her eyes, because by the time I sit down she's looking at me, fierce and very much alive.

"Did you find it?" she croaks out.

I'm pretty sure I know what she means.

"Artie's grave. Yes, ma'am, I did."

She grunts.

"You did a good job taking care of it all this time," I tell her. "I hope I can do as good as you did."

"You will. You're a good man, Willie. No matter what they say, you're a good man."

Talk about a sliver of praise wrapped up in a damnation sandwich. I wonder who "they" are.

It could be alleged relatives of mine and of Artie Lee, wondering why his shiftless son never even knew where his grave was.

It could be members of the African American community at large who mistakenly think I've been using my mother's genes to pass for white all these years.

Or maybe they've been talking to my ex-wives. Or any of my bosses. Or the police chief. Take a number. Hey, my current wife likes me. So do my friends. Butterball likes me when I feed her.

All the "they" are more than balanced by Philomena Slade's approval.

It's hard not to look at all those numbers connected to everything that she's hooked up to, the ones that eventually will signal "game over." Right now, though, she seems alert and up to a few questions.

"Momma Phil," I say, "there's things I don't understand about Artie Lee."

She sighs.

"Things none of us didn't understand."

"Can you tell me about the wreck?"

Her eyes seem to open a little wider.

"What wreck?"

"The one that killed Artie Lee."

"Oh." She tries to sit up a little. I help her with her pillow and make a pig's breakfast out of elevating her bed. A nurse finally comes and helps while making it clear that I am an idiot.

When Philomena's comfortable, I broach the subject again.

She closes her eyes. I'm afraid she's going to drift off.

"That was a long time ago," she says when I'm about to give up on getting an answer.

I tell her what I learned reading the 1961 newspaper article, and what I didn't learn.

"The story in the paper said a boy that saw the wreck said there were a couple of other men there."

Philomena doesn't answer for a while.

"Could've been," she says. "Like I said, long time ago."

"But what did the family say? What did they think? Are any of them still alive?"

I assume they're not, or Philomena wouldn't be coming to me to be Artie Lee's grave tender.

"His folks are all gone," she says. "His two brothers, Curtis and the other one . . . Stump, they called him . . . they both died. They were right much older."

But, I persist, they all were living in 1961.

She nods her head.

"So what did they think? About the wreck and how Artie Lee died?"

"There wasn't much to think," she says. "He was dead. Not much to think about."

I let that sit a bit, hoping to hear something a little more enlightening.

"Artie was always getting into some scrape or another," she says when she finally speaks. "His daddy always said he was goin' to get himself killed if he wasn't careful."

"But did the police ever talk to them, after it happened?"

She shakes her head.

"I don't know, Willie. It was a long time ago. They might have."

"But nobody said anything? What about the boy that said he saw something?"

"Oh, that boy. I do remember something about that. The police must have come by, because Artie's momma, she told me that they said the boy had took back what he said he saw. Said he made a mistake. Oh, and they said they found a half-empty, open bottle of liquor in the car."

I am growing frustrated. Philomena Slade is not a person to accept anything but the truth.

"Didn't that seem wrong?" I ask her. "Didn't anybody think Artie Lee might have had a little help in
getting himself killed?"

Philomena is about as energized as she can be
right now.

"He shouldn't have done what he did," she says.

"What? What did he do?"

She shakes her head.

"All of it."

"Getting a white girl pregnant?"

She looks up at the ceiling.

"That and all the other stuff. Artie had a lot of
friends, they said, but he had a lot of enemies too.
And enemies is harder to lose than friends."

"But who? Who were his enemies?"

She puts one bony hand, the top of it impaled with
a needle, on top of mine.

"It was a long time ago, son. Whatever enemies he
had, they're long gone, just like him."

Philomena is in no condition to undergo the third
degree. I've probably already pushed her harder than
I should have, but she might be the only one left who
can tell me what I need to know.

She shuts her eyes, though, and I figure I'll have
to wait for a better day, if there is one.

Then, as I'm about to sit back and wait in silence
for Richard to return from his break, she speaks
again, with her eyes closed.

"There was one thing that bothered them all
though," she says, so soft I have to lean forward to
hear her.

"Artie didn't drink liquor. Said it upset his stom-
ach. He wouldn't hardly even touch a beer."

—ᴡᴡ—

Unbelievably, the schools are still closed. How are our youth ever going to learn anything? So I have lunch with Cindy and Butterball. Cindy wonders out loud why the cat has become so persnickety about her cat food.

"You haven't been feeding her something unhealthy, have you?" she asks me.

I swear I haven't, and Butterball's not talking.

She says Custalow came by while I was gone and moved a few things in. He told Cindy that he and Stella Stellar probably weren't going to be seeing much of each other from now until she and the rest of Goldfish Crackers hit the road in pursuit of fame and fortune.

"He said he thought maybe she was hoping for some kind of long-term relationship, and he said he wasn't ready for that."

"Well, he's only fifty-seven."

Cindy snorts.

"Too bad he couldn't be like you, Mr. Commitment."

"I just kept marrying until I found the right one."

That seems to be an acceptable answer.

I tell her what I learned from Philomena about my late father.

"Doesn't seem like anybody wants to talk about him," she says. "Maybe you're just tearing off old scabs."

When people get quiet on me, I tell her, it usually means there's something they're not saying.

"Or, it was a long time ago and nobody's even thought much about your father for the last half century or so. Including you."

That could be, I tell her, but I'm a long way from conceding that point. I still have to find the other member of the Triple-A boys. Maybe Archangel Bright can tell me something nobody else has been able to.

I feel the way those people must feel who spend half their lives on Ancestry.com. One of the editors at the paper claims she's traced her family all the way back to Pepin the damn Short. Of course, Ray Long on the copy desk pointed out that there probably weren't but about fifty people alive then anyhow, so we all have a famous ancestor if we look long enough.

Hell, I'll settle for answers one generation back.

—⚶—

I still don't have a Morgue Report offering for Sunday, so I go in to work an hour early, rewarding myself for this devotion to duty by stopping by Penny Lane for a beer that turns into two. By the time I check in, it's regular check-in time anyhow. The road to hell and all that.

It's supposed to be subzero cold tonight, so I start looking for a January 7 in Richmond's past that was cold enough to freeze the balls off a brass monkey.

"Balls off a brass monkey? Where do you get that shit?" Sarah Goodnight asks when I verbalize my quest. "That doesn't even make any sense."

Yeah, I concede, but it made you laugh.

I do find a night, before I was born, when we had a story in the paper on record-breaking if not ball-breaking temps the night before. The story was dry as dust though.

And that's where I take one of those turns that you come to regret later.

Maybe it was the beer talking, or writing. Whatever, I decide that we need to juice up that long-forgotten January night.

What would it hurt, I ask myself, if I wrote about a farmer out in Buckingham County who discovered that one of his cows had wandered out on a frozen farm pond on his property and had fallen through? Hey, it could have happened.

In my breathless rendition, the cow is standing shoulder-deep in the freezing water. The farmer gets a couple of neighbors to help. They crawl out on the ice as far as they dare go and manage to put a rope around Bessie's neck. They tie the other end to a pickup truck and try to pull the animal to safety.

Instead, the cow manages to pull the truck onto the ice, where it sinks. In the end, it's a happy ending for the bovine, who works free of the rope and walks to shore, and a not-so-happy one for the farmer, who says that he guesses he's going to have to get a bigger truck.

To cover my tracks a bit, I note that, in that long-ago story, the farmer did not want his name published because it was so embarrassing.

"Not bad," Sally says when I hand in my opus.

I think briefly about telling her it's just a joke, and that I'll write something drier but truthier. It's just too damn tempting though. I would rather give up Millers than fudge the facts on a real news story. The Morgue Report, though, offends me. It would offend me if someone else was doing it. It's a cheap way to fill space that could have been used for legitimate, happening-now news. The fact that I'm doing this crap, that this is where an adult lifetime in this business has brought me, offends me even more.

The rest of the evening goes as well as a night like this could go, meaning that I did not have to put on my overcoat like last night and report on someone's untimely demise.

I call Cindy at eleven. She says she and Abe are watching an old movie.

"Has anything blown up in it so far?" I ask.

"It's not that kind of movie. You're such a troglodyte. And Abe seems to like it."

"He's lying."

"Anybody kill anybody tonight?"

No, I tell her. It's so boring I've started making shit up.

CHAPTER EIGHT

Sunday

The hawk might be in for a long wait for breakfast. Even the pigeons and squirrels seem to be staying indoors.

The weekend weather guy says it got down to minus three last night. I don't doubt it. It took four tries to get my faithful Honda to start in the company parking deck.

The local TV folks follow the weather with a video shot at the abandoned courts building the city provides for people who don't have access to a roof and walls. Some of the hapless inhabitants are trying to sleep sitting up in hard, wooden seats. One of them says a guy he knows froze to death last week rather than stay there.

Custalow is in the big chair in the living room, taking in the park. Cindy is over at her mother's in Oregon Hill, making sure the old lady didn't turn into an icicle last night. I asked her to drop in on Peggy and Awesome too. She's going to meet us at Joe's later for the Hill gang's usual liquid brunch.

I never ask Abe much about his footloose and home-free days before we reconnected a decade ago, after I found him spending his daylight hours in the same park he's staring at now.

"Must be a bitch," I observe. "What did you do, on days like this?"

Custalow shifts his big body a little, not looking back.

"There always seemed to be somewhere," he says. "It wasn't easy though. And those shelters, man, until they develop smell-o-vision, you won't get the full effect."

There isn't any graceful way to phrase what I want to ask. I put my faith in our long, long friendship, one that I hope gives me a free pass to pose nosy-ass questions.

"How did it happen?"

He understands: How did a guy like Abe Custalow, with a strong back and stronger work ethic, wind up doing minimum-wage day labor, living in a city park and homeless shelters? Even with his prison record, it's always puzzled me. We might have talked about it a little right after I brought him in to live with me, but the subject was kind of like a wound that has healed over and disappeared.

"You had to be there," is all he says at first.

The only noise for a minute or so is the weekend anchor girl, who looks to be about sixteen, narrating a piece on adorable pooches falling on their adorable little doggie asses on the frozen pond at Fountain Lake over at Byrd Park.

"Nobody wants you," he says finally, "and after a while, you start believing that, if that many people think you're shit, you must be."

He talks about the job interviews where he'd have his earthly belongings in a sack that he'd have to set beside the chair while some very uneasy interviewer asked questions and then told him they'd get back to him later. An honorable discharge from the marines

didn't seem to trump his prison term for unintention-
ally killing a man who had been fucking with him.

"No cell phone, no car, no bank account. I was
radioactive, employment-wise. Willie, I was about as
invisible as a man could get without disappearing
altogether."

He wasn't homeless for more than a year, but he
says that another year might have broken him.

"Awesome is lucky," he says, referring to Mr. Dude,
whose own peripatetic life was changed by my mother's generous spirit. "So am I."

I tell him to shut the fuck up.

For two guys from Oregon Hill, that was about as
close to Feelings with a capital-F as we're likely to get.

—⁓—

CINDY IS already at Joe's when Abe and I get there, as
are her brother, Andy, and R.P. McGonnigal. There
used to be six of us, back in the days of our mis-
spent youth: Andy, R.P., Abe, Goat Johnson, Sammy
Samms, and me. Sammy, young and stupid like the
rest of us, didn't make it to thirty.

Goat is still with us, in spirit at least. He's now
Frances Xavier Johnson, president of a liberal arts
college up in Ohio that should know better.

As soon as we get there and order the first round
of cheap Bloody Marys, R.P. puts in a speakerphone
call to Ohio.

"Just wanted to let you know," he says when Goat
answers, "that it's sunny and sixty-five down here.
How is it up there?"

"Bullshit. I do have Internet access. You boys have
it worse than I do. At least we expect blue northers
up here."

"People in hell expect heat waves, but they probably don't like 'em either," Andy observes.

In answer to Goat's queries as to our general well-being, R.P. tells him that I've found my long-lost father.

This confuses our old friend.

"I didn't know . . . I thought Willie didn't have a father."

Everybody's got a father, I inform his eminence. "Some people just don't know where the old man is."

"But, he's not . . . I mean, he's not alive, is he?"

I fill Goat in on my late father's current residence at Evergreen Cemetery, and advise him not to ask me why the hell I didn't know about this until now.

After the usual bullshit and the assurance that Goat will be visiting our fair city sometime soon, we wish him well and promise not to post any of the incriminating photos we have of him, at least for now.

"Assholes," he offers as a benediction. The waitress brings us another round and asks if we might also want food.

With some prompting, I fill them in on what I know so far. Artie Lee was maybe a bit of a troublemaker. ("Apple didn't fall far," Andy observes.) His fatal accident might or might not have been as accidental as it's been portrayed. The kid who said he saw two men changed his story later. Neither Artie's long-ago friend Arthur Meeks nor Philomena Slade seems to want to share much about old Dad. Same goes for Peggy. I relay Meeks's observation that sometimes an accident isn't an accident.

I tell them what a mess the cemetery is. Abe, R.P., and Andy all say they'll go out and help clean up the grave site.

"Hey," R.P. says, "there were times I kind of envied you, not having a dad around to whale on you."

Yeah, R.P. and his dad had what you might call a thorny relationship, especially after the old man figured out R.P. was playing for the other side, sexual orientation-wise. He says they're better now, which just means they don't talk about R.P.'s private life on the rare occasions when they're in the same room.

The guys are as happy as I am to have Abe back in our midst. This is his first appearance at our Sunday morning gatherings since his son's death. R.P. and Andy tell him how good it is to see him, without mentioning anything about his loss. They're going easy on the wisecracks, like they're afraid Abe might break or something. I'll know all's right with our little world when they can give Abe shit just like old times.

Andy comments on this morning's Morgue Report.

"I think that's the best one yet," he says. "I loved the part about the farmer saying he'd have to get a bigger truck. It's almost like that line in *Jaws*."

Yeah, I'm thinking. Art imitates art.

"As a matter of fact," he goes on. "I think you should just quit covering night cops and do this full time."

"That way," R.P. adds, "you can write about dead people without having to actually go and see the bodies, which has got to be icky as hell. And the hours are better."

Please, I implore them, don't mention that bright idea to my publisher.

It's probably still in single digits when we give up our table sometime after noon, so the long-suffering wait staff can wipe it down and give it to the church-goers who are starting to stream in. The Bloody Marys, cheap as they are, make up two-thirds of our bill.

Our waitress tells us to have a good day and, for some reason, advises us to drive safely.

"Wanna go for a ride?" I ask Cindy as we hustle into the car.

"Where?"

"I need to see a man who might know a man who might have known Artie Lee."

"That sounds like a hot tip," she says, wrapping her scarf rightly around her neck, "but, sure, why not? It's a nice day for a drive."

Custalow asks us to drop him by the Prestwould, where he's still unpacking.

The person I need to see is a man named Charleston Bright. Having failed to find Archangel Bright in any Internet listing, I went to our electronic archives, of which I am becoming too familiar. When I typed in his name, I got one hit, in a story about the afore-mentioned Charleston Bright. I know where Charleston lives, or at least did as of three years ago. That was when he made the paper because a tree fell on the street in front of his North Side home, over east of Chamberlayne, and totaled his new Buick LaCrosse. I was able to get an address.

In the story, he's quoted, as is his father, who was visiting.

"If we'd got here five minutes later," the father said, "we'd all be dead."

The father's name was Archangel Bright. Can't be many of those running around Richmond.

With Cindy giving directions off the city map, we find the address. I'm sure it's the right place, because the stump of the Buick-killing tree sits there in the small front yard. I always marvel at how often trees fall away from houses, although I doubt Charleston Bright was feeling too lucky on that day three years ago.

Another car, no doubt the Buick's successor, sits by the stump. We scurry to the front door and ring the doorbell. It takes longer than I would have liked for someone to answer. The woman on the other side of the door doesn't look like she was expecting company and doesn't want any. Plus, Cindy's white and I'm passing, and white folks probably don't come to this neighborhood that often unless it's to deliver bad news of one kind or another.

I try to explain the whole, convoluted tale, boiling it down to this: Charleston Bright's father knew my late father, Artie Lee, who died fifty-seven years ago, and I'm just trying to find out a little bit about him.

The woman, who turns out to be Mrs. Bright, looks at me and seems to doubt that I could be the son of her father-in-law's good friend. She seems on the verge of leaving us out in the cold when we hear a voice from the interior, from which enticing aromas tell me we've interrupted Sunday dinner.

"What do they want?" the voice demands.

"Something about your father," the wife shouts. "And some man named Arthur Lee."

"Artie," I tell her.

"Artie Lee!" she shouts.

I apologize for interrupting their dinner. I hear a chair being pushed back from the table, and then Charleston Bright himself appears. He looks to be in his mid-fifties, heavy and short. He still has on his church clothes.

"What you all want?" he asks, and I repeat the whole thing again.

He must think this is too weird a story to be made up by a bill collector or insurance salesman.

"Come on in, then," he says, "but make it quick."

He gives a glance back at the roast I can see at the table, and the four other people, probably kids and/or grandkids, who are glowering at us for interrupting their meal.

I tell him I just need to know how to get in touch with Archangel Bright.

"And you say you're that Artie Lee's son?" he says, giving me the once-over.

I feel compelled to tell him that my mother is of the Caucasian persuasion.

"Well," he says, "that'd explain it then."

And so he gives me his father's address.

"But you won't catch him there today."

Archangel "Arkie" Bright is spending Sunday up in Fredericksburg with his sister.

"He drives up there almost every Sunday," his son says. "Believe, me, it's a good reason to stay off I-95 on Sundays."

He assures me that his father always comes back on Monday mornings though.

I tell Charleston Bright, as we're about to make a dash back to the car, that I'm sorry about his Buick.

He seems mystified, then remembers.

"Yeah," he says. "I haven't trusted Buicks since then. Bad luck."

Back in the heated car, Cindy asks, "So this guy, Archangel Bright, he's going to tell you all you want to know about your late father?"

"If he tells me anything, I'll be better informed than I am now."

Cindy has never asked me much about my father, understandable since I had hardly ever mentioned his name to her until Philomena Slade forced me to concede that I was not immaculately conceived, that there was a father involved, if only briefly.

"Can you remember anything at all about him?"

I start to tell her that I don't, but that might not be completely true.

"There was something," I tell her. "Peggy might have taken me with her one time, to see him. Or maybe I just dreamed it."

There was a house, and there were a lot of African Americans in it. On Oregon Hill, I might not have seen a black person before, so we must have been somewhere else. I just remember the house, and a man holding me. And me being scared, crying. Like I said, it could have been a dream.

"Aww," Cindy says, the same "aww" she lavishes on babies and puppy dogs. She reaches over across the console and rubs my neck.

I point out to her that I'm not really that emotionally involved in the whole Artie Lee memory chase. It's just a good story, and the fact that it involves my long-lost father is incidental.

"Bullshit."

I tell her that I intend to talk with Mr. Archangel Bright tomorrow, and that she's welcome to come with me. She reminds me that tomorrow is Monday, a school day.

Surely, I say, there must be a patch of ice somewhere in the city whose existence would make it foolhardy to let school buses haul their precious cargo. We've talked before about how ironic it is that, on snow days, the theaters and malls are full of teens who drove themselves there, bravely defying death.

The logic, Cindy says, is that if they kill their own damn selves on an icy road, the school system can't be held liable. Lawyers, what would we do without them?

We spend a quiet Sunday afternoon, with Abe and me watching the NFL playoff games and Cindy looking at porn or whatever the hell she does on her computer.

The second game has just started when Richard Slade calls.

"I thought you'd want to know," he says. "Momma's taken a turn for the worse. She's not responding or anything."

I thank him and say the usual inane things you say at a time like this.

At first, I think maybe Philomena has passed, but Richard says that she's just kind of in her own world, breathing but that's about it.

"They keep asking me about that living will," he says. "I told them there ain't no damn living will."

I tell him I'll be there in half an hour.

Cindy and Abe both volunteer to go with me, but I'd just as soon do this one solo. I haven't seen Philomena Slade enough since we got to know each other through Richard's travails, and I wish I'd seen her more. It is a feeling I often get when I lose or am on the verge of losing someone I care about. Too little, too late. That'll be my epitaph.

If I expected a horde of concerned medical professionals to be hovering around Philomena at the hospital, I am mistaken. When I get to the room, it's just Richard, sitting at bedside, looking sleep-deprived and gut-shot.

His mother lies there, here but not here. She blinks her eyes once in a while, but that's about it.

"I really thought she might pull through this," Richard says when we step outside, in case Philomena can still hear and process what other humans are saying. "But then, I went down to get some breakfast this morning, and when I came back, she was like this. I wasn't gone but twenty minutes, I swear."

It's like he's blaming himself, like he could have pulled his mother back from the edge of her coma, or gotten a crack team of specialists to rush in on a moment's notice. There is no crack team here today. If you're going to need a quick save at a hospital, try not to pick Sunday for your crisis. You could fire a gun down the hallway here and probably not hit a medical professional.

"The doctor did come in, about an hour ago," Richard says, "but he said there wasn't nothing they could do, that they'd just keep an eye on her to see if her condition changes."

I'm thinking, from what I'm seeing, that any changes Philomena undergoes from this point on won't be for the better.

I don't tell Richard that, of course. I do urge him to go get some sleep. He looks like death with a hangover. He shakes his head and says he'll be there for the duration, that they said they could maybe get him a cot or at least a recliner.

"Chanelle comes in once in a while," he says.

"I aim to be here," he adds, when we're about to go back in, "until the end." He kind of chokes on that last word.

He does agree to let me spell him for a few minutes, but only when I solemnly promise that I will call him if anything changes.

The room is quiet except for the beeps and hums of the various machines that are keeping Philomena alive, or at least monitoring the grim reaper's progress. She looks at peace. Part of me thinks this isn't a bad way to go, if this is last call: no apparent pain, no lingering illness beforehand.

Selfish bastard that I am, I am thinking about another kind of loss too. Philomena is, or was, the one link I was counting on most to finally tell me more about Artie Lee. She was his cousin. She grew up right across the road from him and his family. I figured that, given enough time, I could coax more details from her, that I could find out why everything about my late father is such a big damn mystery.

More time, as any fool knows, is something you can never depend on.

CHAPTER NINE

Monday

I take Belvidere south, across the James. I turn right on Hull Street and then left on Broad Rock. Along the way, I pass the remnants of Manchester, a city in its own right until it agreed to be swallowed up by Richmond more than a century ago. North of the river, the old-timers call where I'm driving now Dogtown. They pronounce it "Dogue-town."

Most of the shops here are long gone. The buildings remain, which makes it worse, like leaving a dead man's corpse to rot in the open. It's a place where about the only viable businesses seem to be the Dollar General store and a funeral parlor. Even a 7-Eleven building I pass has been converted into an even less-fancy convenience store, one with bars on the windows.

There are parts of Dogtown that are being gentrified, first by the artists and then by VCU grads looking to stay in the city. They have cool views of our downtown skyline which, situated on a hill, always looks bigger than it really is.

Where Archangel Bright lives is not one of those parts.

Here, people with more time than money hang out at neighborhood stores or on rotting-out front porches.

The ones who can afford it have some kind of home security system.

The street where I find what I hope is Archangel Bright's house is just off Broad Rock, not far from the VA hospital. It's a wooden, one-story abode in need of a new roof and a paint job. A window air-conditioning unit sticks out of the one part of the house that won't be hotter than the hinges of hell come summer. An oil heater sits between the house and the one next door, in the side yard.

I stub out my second Camel of the day and walk up the steps to his front door.

The man who eventually answers my knock appears to be older even than either Arthur Meeks or my late father. As with Arkie's house, it's hard to tell. Maybe he's just had a rough life. He drags his right leg like maybe he's had a stroke at some time in the past, and his right hand trembles when he leans against the doorframe. He also has on Coke-bottle glasses, and he's shrunk a bit from the man in the photo I copied from Meeks's album. The fact that this man reportedly drove one hundred-some miles on I-95 yesterday fills me with wonder.

"Got to get them cataracts done," he says. "The VA says they're not ripe yet."

He seems affable enough, at least compared with other African Americans from whom I've tried to extract information about my late father recently.

"Yeah," he says, in a croaky, high-pitched old man's voice. "My boy said you was coming over. Said you was asking about Artie Lee."

He looks me up and down after he's ushered me into his living room.

"Yeah," he says, "I do see a little resemblance there. There's a little bit of your daddy in you. You're a little paler though."

Arkie Bright seems happy to talk about my father, up to a point. He tells me about the R&B bands he and Artie Lee played in, how they would go to white boys' fraternity parties in Charlottesville or at Randolph-Macon or Washington and Lee.

"Artie, he could play that tenor sax. One night, we was at some club out in the country, over around West Point, and he got up on the beams of this old clubhouse and hung upside down and just kept on playin'. Place went nuts."

I find it to my advantage to let Mr. Bright talk, figuring his rambling reminiscences will eventually close in on something I haven't been able to glean from anyone else so far. Actually, it isn't the worst way to spend a morning, sitting warm and cozy near the heater and listening to an old soul like Archangel Bright talk about days long past. I don't read the obituaries every day, but I confess that I do look at them more than I used to, and I've come to the conclusion that damn near everybody has a story to tell.

Arkie sure does. He seems to have some of the dates mixed up, but I don't correct him, and there's no doubt that time has sprinkled some pixie dust on some of his stories, tweaking and perfecting them so that the memory is probably a little better than the event itself was. Hey, everybody has a little bullshit in them.

Arkie says he was in the army in Korea, which tells me he either disremembers or is a bit older than my father would be.

"Played in the band," he says. "But when we got over there, they give me a gun and sent me out there with the rest of 'em. Like to of froze to death."

He says he and Artie Lee grew up in the same neighborhood "but we was a few years apart," confirming my suspicion that Arkie might be closer to eighty-five than eighty.

"When I got back home from the army, him and some other fellas already had started a group, doing dances here and there. And when they knew I could play a little guitar, they asked me to join them."

He said they all had day jobs "cuz nobody could make a living at doin' music back then, at least nobody black."

He was a waiter and then got on at the bakery where they made the Girl Scout cookies, where he says he worked for thirty-five years.

"Some of them groups playing now," he says, "they don't have any of the old guys there anymore. More like their grandsons. The manager, he'd get control of the name and just bring in new guys. So I hear about bands that we knew of back then, they go to those same college towns, and them white college boys are grown men now, rich and fat, just dyin' to be young again for a couple hours, and they pay them bands fifty times what we got back in the day."

I ask him what their band was called.

"We was the East Enders, to start with," he says, "but then we changed it to the Moonlights. We named it that because we passed a drive-in theater by that name, and Artie said we ought to call ourselves that. Silly name, ain't it?"

I tell him that it isn't the silliest band name I've heard of this week.

When I steer the conversation toward my father's demise, though, Arkie starts playing his cards a little closer to the vest.

"Yeah," he says, when I bring up the wreck that killed Artie Lee, "that was a mess, a real mess."

Yeah, I interject, but how exactly was it a mess, other than being your basic car-hits-tree fatality?

"Aw, you know. He wasn't but, I think, twenty-three. I bet you didn't even know him, did you?"

I explain that I was barely walking when he died.

"But what happened? I mean, I went back and read the story in the paper, and it said some boy said there were two other men there, but he was the only one in the car when the cops got to the scene."

Arkie asks me if I want some more water. I decline, wishing he'd up the offer to at least a beer.

"See," he says finally, "the thing is, it was a long time ago, and I don't remember the details all that well."

I don't mention that, up to this point, a faulty memory hasn't kept him from talking his head off.

"There's some things," he says, "that maybe it ain't that good to remember anyhow. Just brings back bad feelings."

"But what kind of bad feelings?" I feel like I'm trying to catch a cloud.

"Have you talked to Arthur Meeks?"

We seem to be going in a circle.

"What did people say, back then? Didn't anybody in my father's family demand to know what really happened? Didn't anybody go to the police and ask them to investigate?"

Arkie Bright just looks at me.

"Son," he says, "do you know how much damn attention the police would've paid to a black person demanding anything in 1961? There's wasn't any 'demanding' to it. You just took what they gave you."

I ask him if he knew anything about the boy who said he saw the accident.

"That's a long time ago. We heard that the boy went to the police station, and by the time he came out, he hadn't seen a damn thing. I expect all them white cops showed him how he hadn't seen what he said he saw."

At least Arkie remembers that there was a boy.

Like a beagle trying to open a refrigerator door, I persist.

"You know the cops said there was liquor in the car, and that he'd apparently been drinking?"

Arkie looks surprised.

"They did? I didn't know that. Hell, Artie didn't drink. They must of been mistaken."

"Or just made it up."

He doesn't respond to that.

"Did my father have any enemies?"

Arkie smiles.

"Oh, yeah, Artie had a way of pissing people off. He wasn't what you would call subtle. If something hit him wrong, he told you about it. Artie didn't take no shit off nobody, no matter what color their skin was."

"But did he piss anybody off enough that they might have wanted to do him harm?"

The old man gets up now, a process that takes some time with the bum leg.

"Son," he says, "I've enjoyed talking with you. It's good to know that Artie Lee's boy is doing so well out there in the big world. But I'm kind of tired now."

I interpret that to be a polite way of saying, "Get the fuck out of here."

There is no way I'm going to get more from Archangel Bright today. Small steps, Willie. I ask Arkie if it would be OK if I came back and visited with him again, and he said that would be fine.

Why, I ask myself, am I wasting a perfectly good day off chasing my tail? There is every reason in the world to believe that Artie Lee ran off the road, for whatever reason, hit a tree, and that was the end of Artie Lee.

But when there's this much hemming and hawing, dancing around the issue, my radar says something's hiding in the bushes.

—ⱨⱨ—

I GO home long enough to feed Butterball, then head back out before the cat can go into her "What have you done for me lately?" mode.

After eating a pastrami and Swiss on rye at Perly's that could have fed two people, I head down to headquarters, hoping for a conversation with L.D. Jones.

The chief is in, but he keeps me waiting fifteen minutes, hoping I'll leave.

When his aide finally tells me I can go in, L.D. sniffs the air.

"Have you been drinking?"

Of course I've been drinking, I tell him. I just had lunch. What did you expect me to drink, water?

He shakes his head and says he hopes I'm not driving anywhere.

Perish the thought, I tell him. I haven't had a DUI in years.

For a while, R.P. would bring his own breathalyzer to Joe's every Sunday, not so much to ensure that we weren't driving drunk, but to see just how damn drunk we were. From that, I deduced that I cross into no-man's land somewhere into the third weak Bloody Mary or after Miller Number Four.

"Have you been able to find out anything about what we talked about the other night?"

"Don't you think I've got better things to do than spend my time on a car wreck that happened fifty-seven years ago?"

I go into subservient mode, the one the chief likes best.

"I know you do," I say, even calling him "Chief." "But anything you could dig up would be helpful. I'm just trying to find out all I can about my father."

"Well," he says, feeling expansive enough to throw me a few crumbs, "I did find out something. There isn't anybody here now that even knows anybody that worked back then, to my knowledge."

He pauses.

"Except for one guy."

I wait for it.

"Me."

OK, that makes sense. L.D. would have been a rookie cop when I was at VCU, in the late seventies, early eighties. It shocks me to realize that we've known each other that long.

"So, you knew guys who were on the force in 1961?"

"There were a few, but they'd be old as dirt by now. I checked on the pension list though."

He reaches into his drawer and hands me a print-out sheet.

"This is all I've got," he says. "These guys might not know a damn thing, and they might've forgotten what they ever did know."

It's a start though. I thank the chief for this rare exhibition of bonhomie.

"Don't get used to it," he says.

"And Willie," he adds as I'm halfway out the door, "go easy on this."

I ask him what he means.

He shakes his head.

"I don't know. But I've heard things."

"Things?"

The chief looks at me hard.

"All I can tell you," he says, "is look at what happened in 1960. Everybody knows it's you doing that 'This Day in Richmond' crap, so I know you're nosing around there anyhow."

I observe that 1960 is 365 days long. What day?

"I can't do everything for you," he says. "And I shouldn't even be giving you that much to work on."

I'm almost out again when it hits me.

"You said 1960. Did you mean 1961?"

"I meant what I said."

The list he gives me isn't that long. Eight names. Those are all the ones from that far back still above ground and drawing a pension.

Most of the names don't mean anything, and L.D. didn't affix any addresses to them.

One of the names, though, jumps out at me.

Edward M. Shaw. I remember Peggy mentioning him the other day in less-than-flattering terms. I have a hunch that I need to talk to Eddie Shaw.

—w—

I SEE that I've missed a call.

"Where's the Morgue Report?" Sally Velez asks.

Shit.

I meant to do the ones for Monday and Tuesday before I left Saturday night, but then I got caught up in actual, twenty-first century news, dirt-nap style. I did Monday's, a heartrending bit from the 1960s on a blind cat that was being led around by a dog. Butterball would be too proud to accept such assistance.

I forgot about Tuesday.

I tell Sally I'd be there in ten minutes. One Camel later, I enter the newsroom, ready to give the paper a little bit of my day off.

Several reporters and editors are standing by the bulletin board that hangs on a post in the middle of the room.

Mark Baer spies me and calls out, "Hey, Willie. Congratulations. You won."

It is almost never good news when Baer congratulates you. From the look of my other compatriots, they are in no mood to celebrate.

When I get close enough to read the damn thing, it's a list of stories and features that graced our paper over the last week. There are numbers beside them. It takes a few seconds to realize that the numbers are the total page views each story has gotten online.

Right at the top, Numero Uno, is Sunday's Morgue Report, the one on the fictional farmer who tried to pull his fictional cow out of the fictional fucking pond.

"You must be proud," Bootie Carmichael says. Nobody can smirk like Bootie.

It has become more and more obvious to us ink-stained wretches that we are being judged not so much on how important our stories are as we are by how many times somebody clicks on one of them.

The murders I covered last week got pretty high ratings. The thoughtful, meaningful piece Sarah Goodnight helped edit and get into print, on how the residents of a city housing project went through the coldest January in years with only space heaters to keep them warm? It led to a high-ranking official's resignation, but it's in the bottom 20 percent.

"I guess I need to start doing something more compelling, like rewriting shit from thirty years ago," Sarah says. Then, seeing that I am standing right behind her, she adds, "No offense."

I tell her none is taken, and that she is more than welcome to glom on to my lucrative sub-beat, starting with a Morgue Report for tomorrow.

"You know I'm not bitching at you," she says, ignoring my offer. "It's just that we don't seem to have any sense of purpose around here. Aren't we supposed to be about something other than turning out click bait?"

Our latest publisher obviously is under the gun to make money, period. So Benson Stine has decided that we rise and fall on how sexy we are to the Web surfers out there. People covering health and human services or city council probably shouldn't expect a raise this year.

I'm not too hip on the stock market, other than how it might affect my 401(k), but it is my uneducated opinion that we stopped being the fourth estate and started being a "profit center" when newspapers went public and began getting their money from investors who have little patience with low profits and give a shit about truth and justice.

"If you're going to be a wiseass," I tell Sally Velez when I walk over to my desk and see that she's about to weigh in on the subject, "you can write the damn Tuesday Morgue Report yourself."

It doesn't take that long to find something acceptable, a memorable University of Virginia basketball game back when there weren't many of those. Eight days into the new year, my standards for "acceptable" already are sinking like a goddamn rock. At least, though, this one actually happened. I'm just hoping the Sunday piece's Number One ranking doesn't bring enough attention for somebody to call bullshit on the drowning cow.

I even find a workable bit of nostalgia for Wednesday, just to stay a day ahead. I'm out of there before five. It's half-price burger night at the Strawberry Street Café, where you barely spend twenty-five bucks for decent burgers and fries for two, plus a bottle of wine that doesn't require a corkscrew. Cindy's a big fan, and after a day of trying to play catch-up with her young scholars after their snow holiday last week, she probably needs a glass or two of cheap red.

First, though, I call Peggy.

"You mentioned Eddie Shaw the other day," I say. "You know, the ex-cop that you said you once asked about Artie Lee?"

Peggy doesn't know what I'm talking about at first. I attribute this to the marijuana aperitif to which she treats herself most nights.

"Oh, that asshole," she says when she remembers. "What do you want to know about Eddie Shaw for?"

I explain that he might be able to tell me more about Artie Lee.

"How the hell would he know anything? And why do you keep harping on that? Just let it alone, Willie."

"Just tell me if you have any idea where he might be living."

My mother sighs and says to wait a second. The second is more like a minute, but when she comes back, she has a number.

"I think he moved somewhere down south of here. His son, Raymond, he still lives over on Pine Street, down close to Holly. If anybody knows where the son of a bitch is, it'd be him. But he ain't going to know anything."

I thank Peggy.

"Oh, I almost forgot," she says. "Andi says her and that what's-his-name—Walter—might be getting married."

I ask a few more questions, along the lines of when and where, but Peggy's a little fuzzy on the details just now.

CHAPTER TEN

Tuesday

Last night, after our cheap burgers and cheaper wine, I was able to get in touch with Raymond Shaw. Eddie Shaw's son lives in the same house where he grew up, Oregon Hill born and bred.

I got the usual result you get when you call somebody's home phone number these days, assuming they even have one. Cindy is after me to drop the landline, but I still get some small peace of mind from knowing that I have a phone that I'm not likely to leave on a bar counter or drop into a public urinal.

Raymond Shaw's phone rang eight times before the recording kicked in. It was not welcoming.

"I'm busy," the presumptive voice of Mr. Shaw rumbled. "If I want to talk to you, I'll call you back."

I left a message, telling Raymond that I was an old Oregon Hill guy who wanted to get in touch with his father, that I would be much obliged if he could give me some contact information for him.

I hung up with small expectations, figuring I'd have to go by the Pine Street address and catch Raymond Shaw in the flesh.

He surprised me, though, by calling back within five minutes.

"You the same Willie Black whose ass I used to kick?" Raymond said when I answered.

Not unless you caught me at a very young age, I wanted to reply. I tended to be the kicker by the time I was in sixth grade or so. It didn't hurt having guys like Abe Custalow covering my butt.

That answer might not have gotten me where I wanted to go though.

"Could be," I said and then repeated what I'd said when I called. I was racking my brain trying to figure out if and when I knew Raymond Shaw.

"Yeah," he said. "You were always hiding from us, down by the river."

Shit. Razor Shaw. He was five grades ahead of me in school, and he and his buddies didn't mind picking on kids who were half their size. Sneaking down to the river, where Peggy had told me not to go anyhow, was always a risk because of guys like Razor Shaw. His late, unlamented cousin David Shiflett Jr. sometimes was part of that same older bunch of assholes who made life on the Hill so interesting.

I remember now that somebody told me later he had more or less nicknamed himself Razor, a self-proclaimed bad ass, but he was scary enough for the likes of me.

I asked him if he still went by Razor, and he said he hasn't been Razor for forty years.

"Somebody said you work for the newspaper, some kind of reporter."

Yeah, I reply. Obviously, Raymond/Razor is not a subscriber, giving him something in common with most of Richmond.

"Pussy job," Razor said. He added that he was working on thirty years at Altria, which is what Philip Morris changed its name to so people wouldn't know they make cigarettes. I told him I give most of my business to R. J. Reynolds, but congratulate him anyhow. I would have figured Razor to put in thirty years in a much more secure facility than a tobacco factory by now.

Eventually, though, he told me what I needed to know. Eddie Shaw married again, after Razor's mother died, to a woman down in Kenbridge. Razor moved into the house where he grew up when Eddie moved.

"Bitch just wants to get his pension," Razor said, making me think Thanksgiving dinner with the Shaws must be an interesting time. "I don't see the old man much."

Eddie Shaw, I learn, is eighty-five.

"He's too mean to die."

He did have a phone number and an address though.

"What was it you wanted to see the old fucker for?" Razor asked.

I told him some bullshit about trying to do a story on longtime Hill residents, how it was in the old days.

Razor seemed to buy it.

"Come by sometime," he said before I hung up. "We can talk about them good old days."

The way he laughed told me what kind of "good old days" he was thinking about. When I said, "Just name a time, Razor," I don't think he knew how to take it.

It would be fun to see Razor Shaw again, preferably in some quiet spot where I had plenty of room and time to reminisce upside his head for a while. I might be past my ass-kicking years, but it'd be enjoyable to try, for old times' sake.

Nobody answered at Eddie Shaw's place in Kenbridge. I put the number in my wallet.

—〰—

Eₐᵣₗy ᴛʜɪs morning, I go back out to Artie Lee's grave. There is still some snow in the woods around the site, and I get mud up to my socks working my way down the hill.

I pick up some of the trash in the general vicinity and put it in the plastic bag I brought along.

While I'm out here, I call Richard Slade at the hospital. He sounds like he's a quart low on hope. I promise him I'll run by there today or tomorrow.

There really isn't anything to do, maintenance-wise, or any real reason for me to be at Evergreen today. It just seemed like something I ought to do. If there's anything more depressing than an abandoned cemetery on a cold, windy January day, I don't know what it is. All around me, as far as I can see, are gravestones, many overturned and half-buried, sitting underneath trees that are as dead as the departed souls they loom over.

I brush snow off the flat stone and wish Artie Lee a peaceful rest. I'm back on the road before ten thirty, which is when I get a call from Sally Velez.

"I filed it before I left last night," I say when I see who it is, fumbling with the phone as I merge onto I-64, assuming she's obsessing about the top-rated Morgue Report.

That's not the problem though. It's something more elemental: We need somebody, or some bodies, to deliver the goddamn paper.

As it turned out, one of the drivers at our printing plant out in Hanover had an accident leaving the plant last night with about ten thousand home delivery papers in the back, bound for one of the distribution centers. He somehow managed to run off the access road and into a grove of trees, Sally explains.

"But that's not the bad part."

"He was killed?"

"No. He's fine, I guess. He apparently was able to crawl out of the truck and call somebody he knew to come get him and take him to the hospital."

The only problem was, he didn't think to call anybody at the plant and tell them there was a delivery truck with ten thousand newspapers out there in the woods, waiting to be delivered.

"They started getting calls from subscribers not long after seven, and it was eight thirty by the time they found the truck."

The folks at the distribution center, where the driver was headed, had started looking for him long before then. The distribution center is where the drivers wait to get the papers they are paid to deliver. Each driver delivers a couple of hundred or so, doing it basically the same way they've been delivering newspapers since the nineteenth century, except with cars instead of horses and buggies.

The people who deliver our papers don't really work for us. They are private contractors, because you don't have to give benefits to private contractors. They're mostly adults working their asses off at two or three jobs, and if the papers don't get to the distribution points in time for them to deliver them, they have to move on to that second or third job. Since they don't get the aforesaid benefits, they are not overly motivated to show up two hours late for those other jobs because we fucked up.

"So we need people to deliver papers," Sally says.

My inclination is to tell her that I'm not a damn paperboy. I graduated from that job when I was fourteen.

The problem is, if I don't show up, some other poor schmuck, in the newsroom or advertising or circulation, will have to do it, and I am relatively close by, actually no more than five minutes from the paper. I take the Broad Street exit.

By eleven A.M., Chip Grooms and I are in a company car, driving to one of the centers and then getting loaded up with papers. I am only vaguely familiar with the neighborhood to which the circulation manager has assigned us.

"Drive or throw?" Chip asks.

I choose throw.

We find the neighborhood and start the process. I'm trying to read the numbers on mailboxes and constantly telling Chip to slow the fuck down, with middling success. Like me, he has other things to do than deliver newspapers.

Most people in the neighborhood don't have paper boxes, and before we're done, it doesn't matter if they do or not. I am fairly certain that a dozen or so subscribers didn't get their papers, and a dozen or so nonsubscribers did. Hell, we did the best we could.

"Fuck 'em if they can't take a joke," Chip philosophizes.

We're back by one thirty, ready to start the part of our work day that doesn't involve delivering the rag we produce.

Everyone in the newsroom is exchanging war stories. Apparently Chip and I were far from the most hapless delivery tag team out there.

Enos Jackson and some guy from advertising took out a mailbox somehow on the North Side. Bootie Carmichael and Becky Whitehouse finished their route with twenty papers left over.

Our intrepid publisher, we understand, was part of a two-person clusterfuck that delivered a dozen or so papers to the wrong neighborhood, somehow confusing "East" and "West" on the street names.

"You know," Sally says, "the people who do this, they drive and deliver both, one to a car."

I observe that we don't pay them enough.

"If we paid them more," Sarah Goodnight says, "maybe they'd tell somebody when they wreck a truck."

—ɯ—

It's the kind of day where you wish that nothing else will happen. That wish, in my experience, seldom is granted.

Instead, I have to check with the cops on a hit-and-run fatality that happened sometime after two this morning. A VCU student crossing Belvidere got hit by a driver taking a right turn without looking. The driver, kind Samaritan that he or she was, did not stop to inquire about the kid's health, just kept going. They have cameras there, and it won't be long before the bastard is caught, but the pedestrian died, giving chary parents in the boonies one more reason not to send Junior or Missy to school in the middle of bad old Richmond—like kids don't get hit by cars in Charlottesville or Blacksburg.

Peachy Love, my onetime compatriot and snuggle bunny and now the cops' chief flack, gives me the information I need and asks me when I'm going to come by for a drink.

"Oh, wait," she says, "your wife won't let you, right?"

She knows that never stopped me in the past, but I think she's just jerking my chain now. There seems to be a feeling among my associates that, with the lovely Cindy Peroni Black, I might finally end my matrimonial losing streak.

No one answers when I again try to reach Eddie Shaw down in Kenbridge.

Between catching up on the hit-and-run and covering a murder on Accommodation Street, which seems
to accommodate more than its share of violence, I
plan to take time to start doing what L.D. enigmati-
cally suggested I do: take a look at what happened in
1960.

I blow through a month of front pages and local
fronts and am developing a headache when I call time-
out and go to 1961, in search of some acceptable nostalgia crap for Thursday. That's when I catch a break.

On January 11, 1961, there's a story on A1 about
an unsolved murder. I almost miss it, because the
people who designed our pages fifty-seven years ago
apparently considered photos or any other kind of art
to be superfluous frou-frou that kept them from jamming at least ten stories on the front page. Old-timers,
when I first came to work here, said proudly that we
were a "writer's paper," meaning that we were grayer
than January in Seattle. Hell, at least they didn't have
to resort to putting ads in the middle of news stories,
one of our more recent ploys to stay above water.

But one of those ten A1 stories jumps up at me,
as much as a story with a one-column hed that reads,
"Slaying/said/unsolved" can achieve verticality.

Thinking maybe there is something there worthy
of Morgue Report status, I read on. And am rewarded.

The story was considerably less wooden than the
headline. It was a follow-up, revisiting the fatal outcome of a 1960 episode in our region's proud racial
history.

There was a Ku Klux Klan rally, not an unheard-of
event in these parts at that time, in a farmer's field
over in King William County. It took place Fourth of
July weekend. Its apparent intent was to let people

who weren't "God-fearing white Christian Americans"
know who ruled the roost.

It ended prematurely, before its cross-burning
finale, because somebody turned one of the Klansmen's cars into an impromptu fireworks display. There
were two people inside the car, a man and a woman
who apparently had decided to set off a few amorous
Roman candles of their own in lieu of watching the
cross-burning. Dynamite and some sort of timer were
involved. The car, it was reported, lifted about twenty
feet off the ground.

The deceased apparently, as much as the coroner
and others could tell, were still wearing their sheets
at the time that the car went boom, which must have
made the hanky-panky a little tricky.

Talk about between the sheets.

In the six months since the bombing, state and
local police had not been able to make any headway
in solving the killings, despite "rigorous efforts." Many
members of the "colored" community had been questioned, the story read, but to no avail. I can imagine, considering the time, that the "questioning" was
somewhat intense.

"We will not stop," the Richmond police chief said,
"until we find the thuggish killers who committed this
heinous crime."

Even though the bombing took place a good twenty
miles outside the city limits, city police were passion-
ately involved in the investigation, for a very good
reason.

The man who was killed, along with his girlfriend,
was one Phillip Raynor, a twelve-year veteran of the
city police force.

I think I've just been saved from going through
eleven more months of 1960 archives.

As much as I want to spend the rest of the evening going back to the events of the July 4 weekend
of 1960, the Accommodation Street shooting drags me
away, and by the time I file my story, I can barely
keep my eyes open long enough to make the ten-block
drive to the Prestwould. Between visiting Artie Lee's
grave, playing paperboy, and putting in a full day at
the office, I need a nap.

I realize that I haven't filed the Thursday Morgue
Report yet. Fuck it. Sarah showed me how to get into
our archives from the comfort of my own home, so I'll
do it in the morning. No dearth of material for this
one.

CHAPTER ELEVEN

Wednesday

It is a blessing and a curse that I can access our archives from home. No need to go into work early, but it also means work has followed me like a stray mutt to the Prestwould. I can't walk out of the newsroom and leave it behind anymore.

I do the Morgue Report piece on the follow-up to that Klan bombing. Then it is impossible not to go back to 1960 and read up on the event itself. Butterball walks across the keyboard twice, perhaps hoping for brunch, before I banish her from the study.

The story captured precious front-page real estate for a week before it was downgraded to the local section.

It happened on a Saturday night, sometime after ten. Despite it being 1960, before computers and all the other wonders that plague us today, there was extensive coverage in the Sunday morning paper. I've been playing newspaper since the early eighties, and I still can't explain how every technological advance seems to make our deadlines come earlier. Half the time, the homicides I post from the night before wind up being read only by our online audience, most of whom apparently stop reading after they've hit the ten-stories-per-month wall and are then expected to pay.

"Bombing kills two at Klan rally" was spread across A1, the kind of treatment the paper at that time reserved for hurricanes and Civil War reenactments. There were about two thousand people at the event, according to the story. The reporter did not see evidence of a counterprotest of any kind. The crowd, he wrote, stating the obvious, appeared to be all white, although it was difficult to tell "because of the sheets and hoods worn by most of the attendees." He added that the Klan seemed to have had an intimidating effect on the local Negro population.

The car that was incinerated was in a grassy area, surrounded by other automobiles and trucks, about one hundred yards from the stage "where the Grand Dragon was inflaming the crowd." I'm thinking the writer must have been proud of himself for coming up with that one on short notice.

The explosion set off a panic. A few people suffered minor injuries. Several other cars suffered extensive damage when the unfortunate DeSoto went airborne, came down, and burst into flames when the gas tank exploded.

Apparently, most of the crowd scattered as quickly as they could, considering that a one-lane farm road was the only exit. The original story did not list the names of the deceased, pending notification of the next of kin. The writer did get one cop who was there in an official or unofficial capacity to say that they were "burned up pretty bad."

From the photo on A1, it was certainly easy to see how that was so. The picture shows a small crowd standing a safe distance from the smoldering ruins, most of them still in their festive Klan regalia.

One guy who identified himself, I swear to God, as the Imperial Kleagle was quoted as saying, "We know the niggers did this, and they know that God's retribution is coming."

The story the next day identified the victims as Phillip James Raynor, age forty-two, of the Richmond police department, and Miss Julia Windham, twenty-two, of Petersburg. The obit on Tuesday listed among Mr. Raynor's survivors a wife and two teenage children.

Throughout the week, more details trickled out. It seems, in my reading, that L.D. Jones is not the first Richmond police chief to sit his fat ass down on any information that might be of assistance to the press. The chief at the time actually invoked "ongoing investigation" three times that week.

One piece suggested that the reemergence of the Klan in the South was the result of "outside agitators" trying to sow discord in an area where "the races long have coexisted peacefully." It was noteworthy that no African Americans were asked to weigh in on that peaceful coexistence.

One of Raynor's brothers, acting as family spokesman, explained the convergence of the two victims in the DeSoto by stating that there had been some lightning and thunder in the area. Phillip Raynor, he said, had offered Miss Windham, who was afraid of storms, shelter in his car.

A check of the weather report for that day didn't mention anything about storms. One bystander, quoted two days later, said, "Well, it might've been heat lightning."

It took the state police until Wednesday to confirm that the blast appeared to have been caused by dynamite and a timer.

There were reports of raids on black families' households in the area and in Richmond, with police assurances that the perpetrator would soon be caught. There also was one sidebar, on Thursday, about a Negro being beaten by whites in Shockoe Bottom, apparently for being black. At least two crosses were burned in two front yards in New Kent. The mayor of Richmond called for calm.

And then, the story did what stories often do when in the hands of our ADHD reporters and editors. It faded away. A search showed that the state police released four updates over the next half year, each offering hope that the perps would be caught soon, but as of January of 1961, the case seemed to have gone cold as a mackerel.

Custalow comes up for lunch while I'm still wading through all this crap, trying to figure out what if anything all this has to do with Artie Lee.

Abe asks me what I'm working on, and I tell him. He says it reminds him of a story one of his uncles told him when he was a kid. The Klan went into some North Carolina county and tried to mess with the local Indian population. The Native Americans ambushed them and sent their asses back into whatever holes they crawled out of.

"Maybe somebody in New Kent took a more subtle approach," he says.

I ask him what's subtle about dynamiting a car.

"You know," he says, "like guerilla warfare. If you're outnumbered, you use any means available."

Well, maybe it got their attention. I don't find any more stories about Klan gatherings after that July Fourth weekend.

—〰—

I REALIZE that I haven't been by the hospital to check up on Philomena. This is probably because I know that no good news is forthcoming there. This is when I most need to show Richard Slade some support, and it's when I least want to be there.

It's almost noon when I get to her room. I'm relieved to see that Richard does have some family support today. Chanelle is there, along with her twins, Jeroy and Jamal. The twins were half-raised by Momma Phil, but they look like they would rather be anywhere else right now. Hell, I can't blame them. What tweener wants to be in an overcrowded hospital room waiting for the grim reaper? The only upside for them, I suppose, is that they aren't in school.

Richard says his mother is about the same. He says she blinks her eyes, and he thinks maybe she recognizes him.

He says he'd like to step outside for a few minutes, and Chanelle says she'll be there, that she doesn't have to be at work until three.

We leave the hospital and walk across the street to where a vendor is selling hot dogs of uncertain provenance.

"I appreciate you coming by," he says. "Momma doesn't have that much family anymore."

I tell him I'm glad to do it. You don't have to be the twins' age to dislike the disinfectant smell and antiseptic feel of a place where life is cheap and you're constantly reminded that we're all hanging by a damn thread. But Philomena Slade deserves attention and respect. She is one of the few heroic people I have known in my life. Newspapers tend to make heroes out of everybody who gets a stray cat out of a tree. If you're an athlete, you qualify if your team or school's

PR folks frog-march you to the hospital to give a dying kid a football.

When Philomena passes, she won't have one of those two-column, thousand-word paid obits that some people write themselves so everyone will know how great they were.

Although, if I have anything to do with it, somebody at the paper will do something to let the world know Philomena Slade was worthy of our attention.

Richard says he has notified the few distant cousins who are still around, although none of them have been willing or able to make an appearance yet.

I tell him, as we sit on the steps of a medical building and spill mustard on our shirts, about what I've learned so far about Artie Lee.

"So neither one of those old friends of his was able to tell you much about the way your dad died? Well, it was a long time ago."

I mention the story I stumbled on, and how it was suggested to me by none other than our fine chief of police that I look into 1960.

"Well," Richard says, "there ain't much I could tell you. That was before my time. I mean, I heard stuff, growing up, people disappearing and such, although I couldn't name one person who just vanished. We were always afraid of the white cops, which was about all the cops there was. That was kind of par for the course if you were black.

"The old folks, though, they seemed more nervous than it made sense to be. I mean, I guess you could say I've got reason to be suspicious of law enforcement, but you can look 'em in the eye now, like you're maybe equal. Momma, though, she told me to never look a policeman in the eye. I think she thought being invisible was the best policy."

Richard admits that his reckless hardheadedness as a kid led him into a situation that wound up costing him half his life.

"Not that I deserved that just for being a fool, but I did draw attention to myself."

It occurs to me that Artie Lee probably was the kind of boy that Richard Slade later was: too proud to bow down.

I go back up and spend another half hour in Philomena's room, but it feels like she's already left it. I might have stayed longer, but three church ladies, longtime friends of Philomena, make an appearance, complaining about the inadequate parking and the inscrutable maze that finally led them to her room.

"Lord," one of them says as she bends down to kiss Momma Phil's cheek, "it's like walking to Egypt."

I take my leave then.

In the car, I call L.D. Jones.

His aide says he isn't in. I ask her, on the odd chance that he might be wandering back into the office even as we speak, to let him know that I've found that thing he mentioned from 1960. She puts me on hold.

To my great surprise, it turns out the chief is in after all. I guess his aide was mistaken.

He seems unhappy to hear from me, like maybe he was hoping I'd give up trying to find a needle in a 366-day haystack. Like that would happen.

I suggest that we grab a cup of coffee. L.D. might want to talk about this outside the confines of police headquarters.

We agree on Perly's.

I get there first and get a spot near the rear. The lunch crowd has thinned, and there's nobody in the booth in front of me. I sit facing the wall. The chief always likes to have the whole room in front of him, like this is Dodge City and he's the high sheriff.

"You ain't going to let this go, are you?" he asks rhetorically when he squeezes into the seat opposite me.

"If you wanted me to let it go," I tell him, "why the hell did you tell me to look into 1960?"

He scratches his neck and shakes his head.

"Let's just say I'm of two minds about things," he says. "Tell me what you know."

I tell him how I stumbled on the bombings. I recount what I think the chief already knows, about how Phillip Raynor and Julia Windham were blown to smithereens when their car got dynamited at a Klan rally. I tell him that, best I can tell, the state police, local police, and Richmond city police were never able to find out who did the bombing.

L.D. sips his coffee, taking his time.

"That's about right," he says.

"So you knew about this."

"Hell, Willie, everybody in uniform knew about this, although most of those who knew are gone. You don't just blow up a police officer and we let it fade away, even if he was wearing a damn Klan robe. Warts and all, he was one of ours."

Everything the chief knows, of course, is no better than secondhand. Like me, he wasn't toilet-trained when all this happened.

He finishes his coffee and declines a refill.

"Look," he says, "I don't want to get personally involved in this. If you were smart, you wouldn't either. I shouldn't have said anything, but he's your daddy. I had a weak moment. Shoot me."

He does make it quite clear to me that whatever else I am able to glean from all this, I'll have to do on my own. His fingerprints, he warns me, had better not be anywhere near it.

I see his point. He might not have the undying support of some of his troops if it was known that he was helping dig up potential dirt on the department. His fellow African American officers, I'm thinking, might be a little more forgiving.

I ask him if there was much racism in the department by the time he joined.

"Not as much, but it was always there, just a little toned down. You know, a black kid does some bad shit, and he's 'nigger' this and 'nigger' that. But then they'd tell me it wasn't about me, that I wasn't one of 'them.'"

He gives me a hard look.

"But we ain't like that now. I want you to know that."

Before he leaves, I tell him that I am homing in on one of the names he gave me.

"Which one?"

"Eddie Shaw. He lives down in Kenbridge."

The chief nods his head.

"Yeah," he says, "he ought to be able to tell you some shit, if he'll talk to you. You going to call him?"

I nod.

"Well, you might be smart not to mention your, uh, racial heritage. Might make it easier for you to get your big nose in the door."

If Eddie Shaw grew up in Oregon Hill when I know he did, he probably wasn't a member of the NAACP. Hell, he might have had a sheet in his closet too. Mr. Shaw probably already knows who I am though: Peggy Black's bastard half-breed kid. Surely his boy Razor has told him who I am by now.

The chief leaves first. As he's getting up, I ask him what he hopes I find.

"The truth," he says.

For once, L.D. and I seem to be on the same side.

—␣␣—

I WOULD have been to work on time except for Butterball.

Custalow calls me as I'm headed for the paper.

"The cat's gone. She must have escaped when I came up for lunch. I swear, I didn't even see her."

He's looked in the usual places, and Abe knows every nook and cranny of the Prestwould.

I tell him I'll be there in five minutes.

There isn't much to do except go over the same places where Custalow's already looked. The creature must have gone down the stairs. Since she's declawed, I'm hoping she has sense enough not to bolt for freedom if she gets all the way down to the first floor. I also hope nobody's witless enough to let her out the front door.

I've been there maybe half an hour, standing in the lobby and wondering how I'll be able to explain Butterball's disappearance to Cindy, when I feel a tap on my shoulder.

I look around and then down. It's Feldman. And he's holding the cat, which is purring like I've never heard her purr before.

"Did you lose something?" he asks. McGrumpy looks halfway pleasant.

"I found her outside my door. She was hungry."

Well, no, she wasn't. Custalow fed her two hours ago, but Butterball can put on an Oscar-worthy performance of "starving kitty" if food is in the offing.

God knows what Feldman fed her to turn him into her BFF.

Hell, I'm just grateful. I thank him from the bottom of my heart. Maybe Feldman should get a cat. He seems almost human for a change.

Just as I'm about to wipe all the bad thoughts I've had about McGrumpy from my memory bank, he reverts to form.

"I'll bet that damn Indian let her out. We never should have let you bring him in here."

I thank him, take possession of Butterball, and leave before the situation deteriorates.

Due to my feline rescue operation, I'm more than half an hour late for work. This shouldn't be a big deal, since I've given the paper multiples of that in free time on both ends of my work day over the past week.

Today, though, my timing sucks.

Unbeknownst to me, Benson Stine has decided that he's had enough of slack-ass newsroom employees not punching the clock in a punctual manner. And we really do punch a clock, another indignity heaped on us in the recent past. Just like working in the mill.

As I prepare to log in, B.S. appears seemingly out of nowhere.

"You're late," he says.

Yes, I tell him, and I'll probably be late leaving, too, and I might be early tomorrow.

"That doesn't matter," he says, pushing his glasses up on his nose. "From now on, you punch in on time or don't come in at all."

I don't know whether to shit or go blind. Our latest publisher can be a pain in the ass, but up to this point he's done it with a smile, killing our spirits softly.

I ask him what happens when we have a shooting fifteen minutes before my shift is over.

"We'll send somebody else," he says, as if there is anybody else to send.

He seems to realize that he's kind of backed himself into a corner.

"Well," he huffs, just before he trundles away, "we're just going to have to work smarter, is all."

If I get smart enough to make time stand still or go backward, I'll be sure to let B.S. know.

Sarah fills me in on what I've missed.

"He called a big meeting in the newsroom, about one o'clock. He said we haven't been meeting our goals, and that we're going to start being here when we're supposed to be here. Oh, and he said that, when we're here, we're going to have to stop all the lollygagging."

"He really said that? 'Lollygagging'?"

She suppresses a laugh, because the publisher is still in the house, over by sports.

Sarah, because she's now an editor, gets some occasional inside info that mere reporters are not privy to.

"I think he got some bad news from corporate," she says. "Circulation's down. Ads are down. The usual crap."

"So he thinks making us punch in to the minute is going to change that?"

Sarah shrugs.

"I don't know what he thinks. But you know how it is. Shit flows downhill, and we're in Death Valley."

There probably hasn't been a month since sometime after the invention of the Internet when the numbers haven't been down. Not likely to be any in the future, either, as far as I can see.

Management's response to inevitability, though, seems to be to blame it on the peons. We suck, so you guys must be lazy or incompetent, or both. It makes me want to ask them how we got so damn stupid when we used to be so smart.

The whole newsroom is in a funk. There's lots of muttering, clusters of folks wishing they had an exit strategy beyond "freelance" or "work on my novel." There are only so many truth-concealing flack jobs out there.

The good news is that Benson Stine is not one to burn the midnight oil, or even the after-dark oil, at the ol' word factory. Someone sees him leave at five thirty on the dot.

I find a passable Morgue Report item, in which a five-year-old girl, on a January 11th back in the early thirties, got hit by a train over at the railroad yard east of town and lived to tell about it. Unlike the depressing reality of night cops, my nostalgia beat is trending toward the happy ending.

It's cold enough to keep the criminals inside and far enough away from each that none of them gets shot before my beat is over. This gives me time to try Eddie Shaw's number again.

This time, Eddie himself answers. I quickly identify myself before he can hang up.

"You're Peggy Shaw's boy," he says. "That reporter."

"Yes, sir."

"Raymond said you were trying to get hold of me. You ain't going to write no bad shit about me, are you?"

He laughs. I assure him that I'm just trying to find out something that happened a long time ago. I told Raymond that I wanted to talk to his old man about

Oregon Hill, but Eddie Shaw doesn't seem to mind that the topic might be a little more wide-ranging.

"Well, hell, if you're talking about a long time ago, I might can help you. I've been around a long time."

I don't want to do this over the phone, where it'll be easy enough for Eddie to hang up on me, and I don't want to drive to Kenbridge if I can help it.

So I ask him if he's going to be up this way anytime soon.

I get lucky. He and his wife are coming up on Saturday.

"She's the only one that can drive," he says. "They took my damn license."

He's going to be at his former home in Oregon Hill. He says I'd be welcome to come by then. We agree on sometime around noon.

"What's this you want to ask me about, though?" Eddie asks. I tell him that it's kind of complicated, that I'll explain when we meet in three days.

"Well, I hope it ain't too complicated," he says. "I ain't too good at complicated."

Sally Velez can't help overhearing the conversation.

"You're still on that thing about your dad?"

I answer in the affirmative.

"Do you think there's a story there? I mean, something you could write about for the paper?"

I tell her that I'm not sure. I tell her about the cop and his girlfriend who were killed fifty-eight years ago, and how their killer or killers were never found.

"But what's that got to do with your father?"

"Nothing that I can put a finger on, but I'm getting a funny feeling."

I mention the fact that L.D. Jones did something completely unlike him when I asked him to help me learn more about what happened to Artie Lee: He actually gave me information, albeit of a somewhat inscrutable nature.

"Sounds like this might be the best Morgue Report yet," Sally says.

I assure her that I wouldn't be putting this much effort into it if it were just another damn nostalgia trip.

Eddie Shaw might be the missing link here, although I doubt he's going to be nearly as talkative and friendly once he finds out the true nature of my visit with him on Saturday.

It occurs to me, as I dutifully clock out right on time for a change, that it's time to pay another visit to Archangel Bright.

CHAPTER TWELVE

Thursday

Chip Marshman and I aren't on anything resembling the best of terms. This is made less uncomfortable by the fact that we hardly ever see each other. I think he's been down here once since the wedding. Maybe young Mr. Marshman thinks his mom married beneath herself. Could be right on that one.

When Cindy left Donnie Marshman, I think their son took it as a personal affront. He was still in high school then. He's out of college now, sans degree. He works for his father, who seemed intent on extending the DC suburbs all the way to West Virginia, one housing development at a time, until the Great Recession kicked his ass. He has, as they say, downsized his operation.

"Chip's a lot like his father," Cindy says. Her tone indicates that she hopes this is something he will outgrow. She feels guilty about having left, though, and I know she wishes things were different.

The way she tells it, the night she got a rather personal e-mail with an X-rated photo attachment that was meant for her husband was the last straw. She told Donnie she wanted him to leave. He said he had no damn intention of leaving, that it was his house. So she took off instead.

Her marriage to me should have made Husband Number One happy, since the wedding was his Get Out Of Alimony Free card. Her big legacy from the Marshman years is the house he enabled her to buy in the near West End, which she has recently sold for about twice what she paid in 2009. I offered to move there, but she said she likes the Prestwould better than the suburbs.

So today the Chipster is paying his mother a visit. She's even taken a vacation day to accommodate him.

"I wonder what Chip wants to talk about," Cindy says as she and I have a cup of coffee and await her son's arrival.

"Maybe he just wants to get a little closer," I suggest, trying to be positive. "I mean, you are his mom."

"Maybe," she says.

Chip arrives an hour late from his Northern Virginia digs and blames it on traffic on I-95. That's always a good excuse when you oversleep, because the trip from DC to Richmond is rarely without a complete dead stop or two along the way. The bed hair is kind of a giveaway though.

He and I shake hands. He seems to have put on twenty pounds in the past year, a discouraging trend I see among young people in general. Neither my daughter, Andi, who is my excuse for an early exit today, nor her housemate, Walter, seem to have succumbed to this so far, but they are the exception.

I hang around for a few minutes, but it's obvious that whatever is on the boy's mind, he'd just as soon I wasn't part of the conversation.

Besides, I have miles to go before I clock in.

Stop Number One is at a coffee shop in Carytown. Andi's meeting me there to explain why the hell I haven't yet heard about her alleged upcoming nuptials. I've called a couple of times and just got the answering machine. The last time, the message said that anyone wanting to reach her should text her. My text was, "Call me, dammit." To her credit, she did.

She's there when I arrive. She appears to be the only person in the joint who isn't using it as an office. Everyone's on laptops, nursing their overpriced coffee drinks, working on the great American novel or pretending to be a Nigerian prince with a million dollars to dispense.

I befuddle the barista by ordering a plain American coffee, along with an apple pastry that was made sometime this week. I treat Andi to something a bit more exotic.

"What's this I hear about you and Walter getting married?" I say, seeing no reason to ease into the conversation.

"Where did you hear that?"

"Where the hell do you think I heard it? From your grandmother."

She shrugs.

"Well, we didn't want to make any big deal about it. We were going to tell you. We're probably just going to get a friend of Walter's who's a minister to do the deed."

"When?"

"We thought sometime in April. Like maybe the twenty-first."

"Sounds like you've planned it out pretty well."

She brushes a lock of her red hair out of her face. I reach over and wipe a dab of whipped cream off her upper lip.

"Don't worry, Dad," she says. "This isn't going to cost you anything. Walter's doing well. We're both making pretty good money really. And you've already paid for college. That's enough."

I tell her we'll see about that, and then I ask her if Jeanette, my first wife and Andi's mother, knows about it.

"Um, yeah, I guess she does."

I should be glad. Andi's getting married which, as long as you made the right choice, probably beats being single, especially if you're raising a kid.

Still, my feelings are hurt. Everyone seems to have known except me. Were they going to send me a postcard from their honeymoon hotel to let me in on the news?

Andi can see that my feathers are ruffled.

"Oh, Dad," she says, reaching across the table to take my hand, "we're just trying to keep it simple. It just slipped out one day when I was talking to Peggy, who wasn't supposed to tell anybody. But she obviously mentioned it to Mom. We don't want a big wedding. We just want to get married."

"So, I guess young William will be William McGinnis in the near future."

"Maybe. But I'm not even going to be a McGinnis."

Andi, she explains, will continue to be Andi Black.

"It was Walter's idea."

And my grandson, I am told, will get to decide for himself what he wants his last name to be. Since William won't be four until June, that decision won't be coming any time soon.

"So, for now, he'll be William Black."

Can't have too many Willie Blacks, I observe.

—⚋—

NEXT ON the to-do list is a trip to the South Side. Arkie Bright should be home today, and I'm sure he wouldn't mind an impromptu visit. I'm assuming my late father's old friend doesn't have a busy social calendar.

I park the car and hope the ne'er-do-wells camped out on the front stoop two doors away drinking 40s before noon don't see much monetary value in heisting a very used Honda.

At the door, Arkie doesn't seem to remember me at first, but when I tell him I'm Artie Lee's boy, it comes back to him. He seems appreciative of the fifth of half-decent bourbon I brought him. He invites me inside like an old friend. I feel guilty for rousing him. With the bad leg, every movement must be an effort. My guilt is somewhat tempered by the knowledge that the man is capable of driving up and down I-95 when he feels like it.

"So, you wanted to know more about your daddy," he says.

I reply in the affirmative.

"Well," he says, "I was looking through some old albums, after we talked the other day, and I found some more pictures of him."

He asks me if I want anything to drink. I decline, neither wanting water nor desiring that he open his new fifth. He goes off to his bedroom and comes back in five minutes with some photographs that I guess he removed from those albums.

He shows me a couple of Artie Lee by himself, and one of him on stage playing the sax at some drunken fraternity party.

Then he shows me the last one.

Artie Lee and Peggy Black.

"Good Lord," is all I can think to say. I realize that I have never seen a picture of my mother when she was that young. The earliest ones I've seen are when she's holding me.

She looks so young and beautiful, a testament to what nearly sixty years or so of life and marijuana will do to you.

"Um-hum," Arkie says. "That's your momma there. Don't know who took it. Must have been at Artie's folks' house."

I thank him for showing it to me.

"You take it," he says. He insists.

As I'm looking at the image of my mother and father one more time, something catches my eye.

"What's that there, on his shirt?"

Arkie leans closer until his cataract-clouded eyes can identify it.

"Aw," he says, "that's just some mess. Artie Lee, he was always getting into something or other."

It's an inscription of some kind across the chest of what appears to be a T-shirt my father is wearing. I have to lean in myself to make out the writing: The Soulution.

"What was that, a band or something?"

Arkie shakes his head.

"Nah, it wasn't no band. It was just Artie Lee's way to saying we had to have a solution. You know, like 'soul' and 'solution.'"

"But a solution to what?"

Arkie Bright squints up at me.

"The solution to the way things was," he says. "See, Artie thought he could change the world, fool that he was."

I don't really need further explanation of what the hell he means by "the way things was."

"Race," I say.

"What the hell do you think? Hell, yes, race. He might of had an easier time of it, might have been able to change something, if he'd been a little more patient.

"But Artie Lee, he wasn't a patient man."

Maybe Archangel Bright has had time to think about our last conversation. Maybe that's why he seems to be at least marginally more willing to extend his reminiscences of my father beyond Artie's musical career with the Moonlights.

I try to ease into it.

"I read a story, looking through old newspapers," I start. "It was about a big Ku Klux Klan rally that happened the year before my dad died, in 1960. There was a bombing. A couple of people died. Do you remember hearing anything about that?"

Arkie is quiet long enough for me to know I've struck a nerve.

"Yeah," he says. "That was something all right. The police was all over our asses after that. If you was black, you was almost afraid to drive anywhere at night there for a while."

I push it a little farther.

"I guess my father wasn't a big fan of the Klan."

He makes a sound like a laugh with a bad attitude.

"You might say that. Hell, who was? We hated those bastards. But most of us wasn't as brave as Artie Lee."

"Brave?"

Arkie is rubbing his hands together.

He looks at me.

"There's some things, young man, that are just as well left unsaid. Let the dead bury the dead, know what I mean?"

I put my hand on his old, bony shoulder.

"Mr. Bright, all I'm trying to do is find out how my father died. I know he didn't drink, but yet they said there was liquor in the car. The story said a boy claimed he saw two other men there, but then the boy recanted it. A man with the police told me to look at what happened in 1960 if I wanted answers, and that's how I found out about that Klan bombing.

"I can't help but think somebody isn't telling me everything he knows."

Arkie clears his throat.

"If you know everything," he says, "sometimes you find out you know more than you want to, like Adam and Eve biting into that damn apple. Now, if you'll excuse me, it's time for me to take my pills."

I can see I've gone as far as I'm going to go today. I thank Archangel Bright for his time and let myself out.

After a run by Buz and Ned's for a barbecue fix, I call Cindy to ask her how her morning with her son went.

"Don't ask," she says, so I don't.

When I get to my desk a full forty-five minutes before I start getting paid, our publisher is nowhere in sight to observe my diligence.

I have an e-mail from Wheelie: See me.

Mal Wheelwright has been our editor long enough to have served directly under four publishers, a fate I would not wish on anyone, even an editor. We started an office pool two years ago as to how long he'd put up with the crap that is part of his job description, including laying off good, talented people and explaining to the subscribers why they are expected to pay more for less. I was down for eighteen months, so I'm out five bucks on that one.

Wheelie's a good man, I believe. In my experience, though, even good men will often do what's necessary to pay the bills.

He asks me how it's going. I tell him things couldn't be better, that I wish they'd let me do two "Today in Richmond History" pieces a day instead of just one.

"I know," he says, letting his body language and eye roll tell me what his mouth can't.

He gets to the point pretty quick.

"You're working on something about your father, Sally tells me. Like how he died or something?"

I hadn't wanted to talk about it with Wheelie just yet. First, I don't have nearly enough to do anything right now. I'm still in the dog-chasing-the-car mode. When I catch it, I'll figure out what to do with it. Second, you can talk a story to death. Just write it, and then talk about it.

Now, I have no choice. When I spell out what I know and what I suspect, it sounds flimsy as a Victoria's Secret negligee. How do a double murder in 1960 and my father's fatal wreck the next year have anything to do with each other?

"I still have a lot of I's to dot and bridges to cross," I explain.

"Maybe you could do something for Father's Day," he says. Sarcasm isn't Wheelie's genre, so I don't take offense.

I tell him that he'll have something by Groundhog Day.

Wheelie leans back in his chair.

"Maybe you ought to ease up on that one a little," he says. "The publisher doesn't think we're getting enough in-depth pieces on the police beat. You know, like overview stuff."

I tell Wheelie what he already knows, that we did an overview at the end of the year on why Richmonders keep killing each other. It's pretty damn simple: poverty and easy access to guns. I also mention that I could turn out an overview a week, if there was material for one, in the time I'm wasting on the Morgue Reports.

"Oh, no, no," Wheelie says. "That's been a real winner. B.S. likes the hits we're getting on that. But he wants to see more perspective from your beat. And it does seem like you're spending a lot of time chasing this story about your father. I understand you were late yesterday."

So I kind of lose it.

It is a dangerous bluff to tell your boss that if he thinks you're not earning your keep, he should just fire your ass, especially in an environment where merely drawing a salary can be a firing offense.

Still, that's what I do.

After I speak my piece, I get up to leave, hoping I still have a job.

"Willie," my editor says, to my relief, "wait a minute. We've been through a lot. We'll survive this. Just work with me. Just be sure nobody thinks you're doing this story on your father on company time."

The "this" Wheelie's asking me to survive, we both know, is the latest publisher, although the real problem, we both understand, is some bastard or bastards sitting in MediaWorld's offices three states away trying to squeeze every ounce of juice out of this lemon before they toss it. If a veteran cops reporter gives them an excuse to cut expenses a bit more, all the better.

I promise Wheelie that, when it comes to the ghost of Artie Lee, I'll do it off the company clock. Of course, my fingers are firmly crossed. Wheelie knows this. His message, received loud and clear: Don't get caught.

By January standards, the city's carnage count is pretty high today. A homicide on the North Side early this morning, a nonfatal near the VCU campus and a body found down by Texas Beach this afternoon, homeless and frozen, keep me hopping.

And, of course, there's the Morgue Report. I keep promising myself that I'll get a day or two ahead on it, but so far, I've let myself down terribly. About eight thirty, between live-time tragedies, I go hunting for a January 13 blast from the past.

This time it's a pet boa constrictor that a knucklehead out in Bumpass was keeping inside his house sometime in the late seventies. In a feloniously careless move, he managed to let the snake, which turned out to be about nine feet long, get away. How the hell do you lose something that big? In any case, one of his neighbors found it. Actually, the snake kind of found him. As the neighbor was opening his car door in his garage, he saw something move down below.

He got on his hands and knees and came face-to-face with the critter, whose name was Lambert. The owner was a Steelers fan.

In the ensuing kerfuffle, the guy, no doubt after voiding his most recent meal, jumped on top of the car and then jumped down on the other side. He ran into the house, got his pistol, and came back out. Goodbye, Lambert.

He should have saved a bullet for the dumbass who let him get away.

Having dispensed with my most important duty of the day, I give Cindy a call shortly after ten.

"So, is it OK to ask now?"

Cindy's had a drink or three, I can tell. She says Abe's out somewhere. Her words are a little slurred, which I find adorable but also a bit disconcerting. She doesn't usually drink alone.

The story, it turns out, is not one to warm a mother's heart.

The Chipster, she tells me, wants to be an entrepreneur. Worse, he sees himself as a restaurateur.

Maybe it's the economy, or just the way so many kids are coming out of college with no job offers that don't require asking, "You want fries with that?" Whatever, a lot of people now think they can operate a restaurant. Everybody who has ever scrambled an egg seems to think it would be "cool" to run an eatery.

I could name two dozen places in Richmond that have been serving me and others well-received meals for the past forty years. Every one I can think of has done it the old-fashioned way: good, inexpensive food, decent enough wages to keep dependable wait staff and bartenders around, and slow, careful growth. None of them are part of chains, and they've mostly resisted the urge to open a second place in the damn suburbs. Before the tobacco Nazis took charge, a lot of them would even let you smoke.

The fancy-ass places, they come and go. Joe's, the Bamboo Café, Chiocca's and the rest built something that would last.

Not surprisingly, Chip Marshman is not inclined to go the slow and steady route. Like his father, from all accounts, he wants it and he wants it yesterday.

What he has in mind is a place that will serve an upscale clientele. He's aiming to give them cuisine instead of food. His place will have your Kobe beef and organic salmon. It'll offer hams from Spain and Italy, when the best ones in the world come from Smithfield, a damn hour away. It'll have quinoa and kimchi. The place, Cindy tells me, will have a wood-fired grill where they'll make pizzas almost as good as the ones I can get from the Robin Inn for nine bucks. It'll have oysters not just from the Chesapeake, which is as close as Smithfield, but from the Pacific damn Ocean. It will, *de rigueur* for joints of its ilk, have a rooftop bar serving drinks so fruity and precious that you couldn't swear they contained alcohol.

So, I ask my beloved, already knowing the answer, what do Chip's plans have to do with you?

Like a shark smelling blood, Cindy's only offspring has learned that she's sold her house for a tidy sum. What he wants from dear old mom is an investment.

"He says if I can just get fifty thousand, he can get it up and running," she says.

Why, I ask, doesn't he go to his father? Donnie Marshman might not be the high roller he was before 2008, but surely he's able to stake his boy to this surefire gold mine.

Or, maybe not. It turns out, Cindy tells me, that Donnie Boy is a little cash-depleted right now. In other words, he's broke. Or maybe he's just telling Chip that because he isn't inclined to piss away fifty thousand dollars on his feckless son.

It isn't even a loan the boy's asking for. He wants to make his mom a partner. How thoughtful.

This gets tricky. It shouldn't be up to the new husband, or at least the new husband with good sense, to tell his new wife that her son is a worthless deadbeat, and that Chip's restaurant probably has a shorter life expectancy than a damn gerbil.

Maybe, I suggest gently, you might put him off a bit, until you've had some time to think about it, meaning time enough to come to your senses.

"Oh, hell no," Cindy says. "I'm not using half my nest egg on some damn restaurant. I told him I'd think about it, because I didn't think I could bear to see the look of disappointment I'd get if I told him face-to-face.

"But then he told me he had to have the money right now, that otherwise his other 'partners' were going ahead without him."

So that's when she told him, flat-out, that she couldn't see her way clear to invest fifty K in a restaurant.

"And that's when it got ugly."

She says Chip told her that she'd never been there for him, that this was like she was abandoning him again. How sharper than a serpent's tooth, etc.

"I didn't work for ten years so that he'd have a stay-at-home mom," she says, getting about as maudlin as an Oregon Hill girl ever does, "while his daddy was screwing the secretary, and he thinks I wasn't there for him."

Long story short, it isn't likely that the Chipster will be spending Thanksgiving or Christmas in Richmond. *Quel dommage.*

Still, you don't stomp on your son's dreams, hopeless though they are, lightly. It is obvious that Cindy will be awake when I get home and that I will need to let my ears work.

CHAPTER THIRTEEN

Friday

We're having our second snow of the new year, meaning that Cindy has another day off.

It's a good day to sleep late. We stayed up past two this morning, drinking and talking about her ungrateful son. She tilted dangerously toward caving and giving him the money a couple of times, but her sage and diplomatic husband managed to steer her back from Crazyville without actually saying that she gave birth to an asshole. The upside of fucking up three marriages is all that hard-earned experience. I could teach a course in What Not To Do 101.

What a crazy thing parenting is. There is damn little correlation between what you invest in it and what you get back.

Cindy puts her teaching career on hold for a decade, goes to all the PTA meetings, works as a volunteer teaching assistant, bakes shit for school fund-raisers, and what does it get her? A son like Chip, whose birthday cards to his mother come a week late, or maybe he'll just call and say he's been "super busy." It gets her a kid who, past the age when he should be a college graduate, only shows his ass around here when he wants to separate her from part of her already too-small nest egg.

I, on the other hand, was the poster boy for negligent dad. People should have egged my car on Father's Day. After I left Andi and her mom for the promise of exceptional sex that didn't even turn out to be that exceptional, I wasn't around much until Andi was in high school. Guilt is about the most acceptable excuse I can offer. But when I started trying to exhibit some small semblance of human decency, Andi was willing to open the door. We had our ups and downs, but we're at a better place right now than I ever had any right to expect. I mean, she named her son after me, sort of.

Long story short, Cindy deserves Andi. I deserve Chip.

The paper will have early deadlines because of the snow, which doesn't mean much to me. Still, an e-mail notifies all newsroom employees that we have to be in at twelve thirty because we plan to lock up the paper by nine thirty tonight. Considering our publisher's recent infatuation with punctuality, I guess I'd better plan on making the ten-block walk to the paper in a timely fashion. Or maybe I'll take a two-minute bus ride today.

In my early days playing journalism, management made allowances for acts of God. If some of us couldn't get in because of half a foot of snow, we still managed to somehow get the damn paper out. Oh, there were slackers, the ones who intentionally parked their cars at the bottom of some suburban hill so they could legitimately claim they couldn't get in. Most of us, though, gave it a good-faith effort. As a reward for that good faith, anyone who didn't think it was safe to drive home could stay for free, meals included, at the Hotel John Marshall, which was a pretty swank joint in its day. I once saw Bootie Carmichael charge three meals, plus drinks, to the paper between eleven P.M. and two the next afternoon.

Well, the John Marshall's been converted to apartments, and if you live out in the boondocks and can't get in, it's on you.

At least snow has a way of tamping down the homicide numbers.

We get up at nine thirty and spend an hour over coffee and scrambled eggs. Custalow's already long since gone to work, trying to help the Prestwould's antique boiler get through at least one more winter.

Sometime before eleven, I get a call. L.D. Jones wants to talk to me. This does not happen very often.

Well, if it's a slow day for police reporters, I guess it's a slow day for cops too.

Perly's is open and crowded when I walk in. L.D. is standing, waiting for a table.

He drove, and he suggests that we just go for a ride instead of having coffee.

We wind up over in a deserted parking lot next to a condo building on the North Side that used to be a hospital.

The chief hasn't spoken more than ten words since we left Perly's. He's silent for another minute or so as we sit there in the idling car, watching traffic creep by on Westwood.

Finally, my silence is rewarded.

"I found out something," he says.

What L.D. has found took a lot of digging. I am impressed that he has put this much time into it, and even more surprised that he's sharing this precious information with me.

"You don't know where this came from," he says. I promise that this will be the case. Whatever the chief might think of me, I don't believe I've ever given him reason to doubt that my word is as solid as a brick shithouse.

L.D. was able to get in touch with one of the other old-timers who were wearing the uniform in 1961, a guy named Jimmy Watts.

"He didn't want to tell me," the chief says, "but once I got him talking, he eventually told me what I wanted to know. I think he was lonesome, just wanted somebody to talk to. Poor son of a bitch is stuck in one of those damn Medicaid rest homes. Place smelled like piss and death."

The retired cop did still have a good memory, though, or at least he talked a good game. When L.D. got him reminiscing about the Klan bombing on the July 4 weekend of 1960, he started in on it "like it was yesterday."

He knew the names of the two detectives in charge of working the case.

"You have to understand, about half the damn force was trying to find whoever did it, but they were the ones that were on it all the way until all the leads went dead. One of them has passed on. You might recognize the other one. It was one of the names I gave you the other day."

Edward M. Shaw. Eddie Motherfucking Shaw.

It seems unfair not to tell the chief that I will be meeting with the same Eddie Shaw tomorrow.

"You don't waste any time, do you?" he says. The way he says it makes me think L.D. isn't all that surprised that I've managed to get in touch with Shaw.

"Well, whatever you tell him, it better not have my name attached to it."

"And they would have been working the case the next year, the year Artie Lee died in that car crash?"

L.D. nods.

"Yeah, and for some time after that, although nothing much came of it, according to old Jimmy."

The heater's working overtime. He rolls the window down a little.

"I started wondering about that kid," the chief says when I think our conversation is over.

"What kid?"

"The one that said he saw the accident."

L.D. Jones has gone to the great trouble of tracking down that long-ago boy.

"There wasn't any evidence of him ever running afoul of the law again. The only thing I could find on him was when he died."

The only known witness to the wreck passed away in 1988, the chief tells me. There didn't seem to be anything unusual about his death, other than it came way too early.

He sighs.

"Too bad," he says. "I know you wouldn't have minded talking to him."

That's putting it mildly.

I feel like I'm in some kind of alternative universe, where our chief of police spends his own time to help me get to the truth, as opposed to going to great lengths to hide it from me.

I'm pretty sure I know the chief's motivation.

"You have to understand," he says, "this is all up to you. I've given you what I can give you. It's up to you to get off your ass and do the rest."

When we get to the bottom, I promise L.D., assuming there is a bottom, no one will be able to find his DNA on it.

He drops me off a block from the paper, a one-Camel walk.

I call the hospital. Richard is, as always, in his mother's room. There's been no change in Philomena's condition.

—⚉—

The paper is surprisingly busy. It appears that most of my coworkers chose braving the two inches of snow over taking a vacation day in the middle of a minor January ice event.

Our publisher is in his element. Benson Stine doesn't know much about how journalism works. He was never a beat reporter or anything else at a newspaper that didn't include wearing a suit and sitting in an office.

Because of that, he has homed in on weather. He seems to think we can win a Pulitzer Prize for our meteorological coverage. The poor guy who was hired to write about it every day is being run ragged. Right now, he's out there somewhere, pestering people who are trying to de-ice their sidewalks and shovel their drives.

How much did it snow in Beaverdam? How about Cuckoo and Central Garage? The publisher's thirst for knowledge about this rather tame little storm probably exceeds that of our readers, but at least it keeps him busy.

"He wants hourly updates on the website," Sarah tells me. "He had me send Baer up to the top level of the parking deck to measure the accumulation. I think it changed like a tenth of an inch in two hours."

God help us all if B.S. is still around when we have our next hurricane.

At least the weather is the jumping-off point for a relevant Morgue Report. I found a January 13th during World War II where we had a real snow. It measured fourteen inches and brought the city to its knees. Unable to help myself, I decide to make the story even better with a heartwarming aside about a paperboy who walked two miles in the snow to deliver not only his route but that of his little brother.

File that one under "Amazing if True."

The publisher reads my daily blasts from the past before they go into print, unless he's already left the building. He is ecstatic. For him, it's a two-fer. It's hard-core weather porn, and it has the added benefit of giving the public a little lesson in how hard their doughty little newspaper is working for them.

Meanwhile, half our readers probably will wake up tomorrow morning to no paper. When they call circulation, they'll get a recorded message telling them what they already know, and that they're welcome to read us online.

No crimes worth my attention occur before our lockup. I regret not driving in today. That ten-block walk over our ancient and uneven brick sidewalks is tricky enough in daylight.

I call Cindy and ask her if either she or Custalow can come get me. She says Abe is out. Stella Stellar is back in town for a night or two in the midst of Goldfish Crackers' first semi-national tour, and Abe and Stella are renewing acquaintances.

Cindy says she's already in her pajamas, but she'll come if I really want her to. I tell her to stay where she is, that she and her pajamas can warm me up when I trudge home.

Sarah asks me why I don't just call Uber. I tell her I don't know how to do that. She shakes her head, as she often does when she's disrespecting her elders, and says never mind.

She gets on her iPhone, and in about two minutes, she looks up and tells me I'd better scoot, that my ride will be there in three minutes.

"You can pay me later," she says.

She's off by a minute. A real estate agent who obviously isn't doing all that well picks me up in his Lexus. Is this a great country or what?

Back home, snuggling by the light of the gas fireplace, I fill Cindy in on my eventful day.

"So the chief volunteered information to you?" she asks, much as she might have questioned a lamb lying down with a lion. "He actually went out of his way to help?"

"Hey," I explain. "You take your tips where you can get them."

I know L.D. has his motives, and that his wishes and mine do not often coincide.

This time, though, maybe they do.

CHAPTER FOURTEEN

Saturday

I have time to pay a visit to Andi, Walter, and young William before my meeting with Eddie Shaw. I'm able to park only a block away from their townhouse, something of a miracle in the Fan, especially with all the unremoved snow.

Walter apologizes to me for not asking for Andi's hand before they decided to make their union legal. I tell him not to worry, that none of my four former or present fathers-in-law were accorded that honor either. If I had asked, at least a couple of them might have said, "Hell, no," and then where would I have been?

Walter is working on his taxes, something that won't be on my to-do list until I can see April 15 on my monthly calendar. It won't hurt, I'm thinking, to mix a little neurotic stability into the Black family free-range chaos. Maybe the fact that he and Andi are getting married April 21 makes him want to clear the decks of less-important matters.

William is playing some video game in which fear-some people seem to be killing each other in alarming numbers.

When I ask Andi if that's really good for a three-year-old, she says it helps his hand-eye coordination.

She adds that Walter is already gently suggesting that they find more educational and less sadistic games for the boy. Good for Walter.

Andi asks me if I've talked with my mother lately.

I tell her that I haven't, but maybe I should. It seems, I snark, that she knows more about certain family members than I do.

"I was going to tell you," she says.

She brushes a strand of her hair out of her eyes. "She's worried."

"About what?" It isn't like Peggy to worry about much of anything. Marijuana makes some people paranoid. For my mother, it seems to be an antidote to stress.

"All the stuff you've been asking about, about your dad."

"Your grandfather."

"Yeah, my grandfather. But she told me that she wished you'd never, as she says, 'opened that can of worms.'"

It is a strange world indeed when L.D. Jones assists me in getting to the truth and Peggy, who normally could give two shits about what I dig into as long as it doesn't endanger me, wants to suppress it.

I promise Andi that I'll stop by and see the old girl today. No big deal, since I'll be in the neighborhood anyhow.

I drive down Laurel past Peggy's place. I'll pay her a visit after my meeting with Shaw.

Externally, Oregon Hill hasn't changed that much since I was a kid and we lived in five or six different places up here, moving whenever the rent went up or the landlord pissed Peggy off in some other way. Oh, it's more Yuppified now, and a lot of college kids rent

there, but you can only do so much with small houses
on small lots.

Back in the eighties, Virginia Commonwealth University lusted after the Hill. VCU didn't want the
houses, mostly late-nineteenth-century wooden struc-
tures built for immigrant factory workers. The school
just wanted the hill itself, overlooking the James, a
perfect setting for its grand plans.

No one suspected that the residents themselves
actually gave a damn about their neighborhood. Before
too long, VCU realized that it had stumbled into a
hornets' nest. It found that poor black communities
were easier to displace than poor white ones.

A couple of blocks down from Peggy's is one of the
newer houses on the Hill. It's new because eight years
ago the original dwelling burned to the ground, taking
David Junior Shiflett and Philippe Ducharme, née Val
Chadwick, along with it. The fire would have toasted
my marshmallows, too, if it hadn't been for the late,
great Les Hacker, my savior and the best roommate
my old mom ever had.

And today I'm having a chat with Shiflett's uncle,
a couple of blocks away. When Faulkner said the past
isn't even past, he must have been thinking about
Richmond in general and my own tangled life in particular. Everywhere I go, history jumps out of the
bushes and nips at my heels. Sometimes it haunts
my dreams, some of which verge on what you might
call nightmares.

Peggy asked me, after Kate and I ended Marriage
Number Three, why I didn't buy a place in Oregon
Hill. God knows the prices are reasonable enough by
Richmond standards.

I told her that I was close enough to the Hill, that
to me it was like a whirlpool, and if I got any closer,

I might drown in it. She took small offense at that, since she's lived here for fifty-eight years.

No offense, I told her. It wouldn't be an unpleasant way to drown. I just want to stay above water, for now.

Raymond Shaw's house, on the same side of Pine Street as Mamma Zu and close enough to make you hungry if you're here around dinnertime, looks pretty much like all the rest. It doesn't appear that my old nemesis has done much in the way of renovation since he took it over from his dad. A rusting Crown Vic takes up most of the space in front. I'm able to park two houses down.

Raymond Shaw answers the door. It's a shock when you see people from your distant past and realize how much you've aged by seeing how much they've aged. The former Razor still has red hair, just now turning to gray, but his face is a road map of a rough life. I think I remember that he tried his luck at boxing once upon a time, and his face backs that up. His nose is cockeyed and looks like somebody tried to push it back into his skull, and there's an old scar on his left cheek that makes me think maybe somebody long ago took a razor to him. Maybe that's when he dropped the nickname.

I remember him as a big boy, but he's a small man, maybe five or six inches shorter than me.

"Willie boy," he says, the good humor in his voice not traveling all the way up to his eyes. "Long time no see. Come on in."

We exchange small, insincere pleasantries, mostly about people we both know or knew. Since he's five years older, there aren't that many points of reference.

"I heard that McGonnigal boy turned out to be a fag," he says at one point as we run down the list of old acquaintances. Nobody has ever wondered why

R.P. didn't move back to the land of his people once he got old enough to leave.

I tell him I don't give much thought to my friends' sexual persuasion.

He shrugs.

"Whatever."

Before he leads me into the living room, where I assume his father is waiting, Raymond pulls me aside.

"You know," he says, "some of us were a little pissed at you, after that mess with David Junior and all."

OK, yeah, I get that. David Shiflett would have been Razor's cousin.

I mention that Shiflett did murder an innocent college girl, and he would like to have done the same to me if luck and Les Hacker hadn't intervened.

"Yeah," he says, "David was kind of fucked up, but still, the way I heard it, you got involved in something that wasn't any of your business."

Maybe Raymond Shaw does read the paper after all.

I explain, as politely as I can, that getting into other people's business is kind of what I do, being a newspaper reporter.

"Reporter," he says, shaking his head. "Tits on a bull."

He leans closer and almost whispers it: "Getting into other people's business can be hazardous to your health here on the Hill."

I'm resisting the urge to further rearrange Raymond Shaw's nose. I think I can take him. But I need to talk to his father more than I need to kick Raymond's ass. Maybe later.

Eddie Shaw is sitting in a greasy-looking easy chair, watching ESPN. I urge him not to get up, because it looks like that might take a while. I pull up a chair, and Raymond takes a seat a few feet away. I was hoping it was going to be just me and Eddie, but no such luck.

"So you're Peggy's boy," he says in a voice that's stronger than the rest of him. "You ain't turned out to be such a ugly man."

I guess it's as close to a compliment as Eddie Shaw's likely to give.

"I still remember you when you was little," he says. "We always said you was the only 'black' kid in Oregon Hill, in more ways than one."

This old, mean joke manages to crack up both Eddie and Raymond.

"Couldn't have been much fun," Eddie says.

"I got over it."

"Yeah, I see you did. So what can an old fart like me tell you? You said you were doing some kind of research about the old days up here."

Not exactly, I explain.

"What I'm really interested in is finding out more about my father, Artie Lee."

The old man looks a little confused.

I plunge in.

"All I knew, growing up, was that he died in a car crash. But now I think I'd like to know a little more."

Eddie gives me kind of a sideways glance.

"Don't nobody know everything. Sometimes it's just as well."

From his body language and the way he's not looking at me straight-on, I'm pretty sure that Eddie Shaw's memory concerning Artie Lee is better than he's letting on.

"But why are you asking me for? All I know is he was a troublemaker that brought a bunch of grief. Hell, he brought enough to Peggy and you."

I point out the obvious.

"I wouldn't be here without him."

The "troublemaker" reference gets my attention.

"I guess you'd know about the troublemaker part. I mean, you were a detective back then. I guess you kept a pretty good eye on troublemakers."

He doesn't say anything. I press on.

"Here's the thing: Something happened the year before my father died, back in 1960. The Ku Klux Klan bombing? And I understand that you were one of the detectives working that case."

The old man's jaw clamps shut hard.

"Killed Phil Raynor, and that girl he was with."

"And you never did find out who did it. At least not that I could find any record of."

Raymond jumps in.

"What the hell has all that got to do with your old man? Why are you asking him about all that shit?"

Just trying to put the pieces together, I tell Raymond. It being his house, or at least the one his father lets him live in, I guess he or his dad can tell me to get the hell out whenever they like.

"You know," Eddie says, "that thing you said about not finding out. You oughta know: When it comes to cop killers, we always get our man."

I tell him that I've heard that. Maybe, I suggest, there was more than what made it to the newspaper.

He chuckles.

"There always is," he says.

Raymond tells his father that it might be time to keep his damn mouth shut.

That has an effect on Eddie, but not the one his son wants. He informs Raymond that he doesn't need anybody to tell him what not to say.

"I give you this damn house," he says, beating on the arms of the chair. "If you don't start treating me with some respect, I'll take the son of a bitch back too."

Raymond gets up. Before he storms off to get himself another beer, he says, "Just be careful, old man. That's all I'm saying."

I go into quiet mode, hoping Eddie will fill the silence with something I can use.

"You know," he says at last, "there was a lot of pressure on everybody to get that case solved. You look back now and think, 'Ooh, the Klan. How evil.' But the Klan did a lot of good, kept the troublemakers in line."

Like my father, I think but don't say.

"Phil Raynor wasn't the only cop that wore a robe once in a while, I can tell you that."

I nod.

"But was there any reason to believe that my father was somehow involved in the bombing?"

Eddie smiles.

"Now why the fuck would you think that?"

"A little birdie told me."

Of course, that's a lie, but the big bird down at police headquarters has dropped me a pretty sizable hint. Sometimes, if an old buzzard like Eddie Shaw hears that another birdie's been chirping, it makes him more likely to join in.

Eddie gives me the fish-eye.

"Little birdie, huh? Well, there ain't many birds still around that know that story."

"But what's the story?"

The old man laughs, which leads to a coughing fit. When he gets his breath back, he looks over at me.

"If I told you," he says, "I'd have to kill you."

Raymond is back in the room now, trying to keep a rein on his old man's mouth without pissing him off again.

I try to coax a little more out of Eddie.

"Did you or any of the other police have run-ins with Artie Lee before any of this happened?"

"Oh," he says, "he was on our radar."

"How so?"

"Like I said, he was a troublemaker."

"How did he make trouble?"

"You know, race stuff. It ain't politically correct to say it now, but a lot of folks back in those days, they didn't think it was right for the races to mix. No offense."

How could I possibly take offense at that?

"It happened so long ago," I say, pushing on. "Just about everybody who knows what happened is dead. I'm just trying to get to the bottom."

"Well," Eddie says, "I ain't dead, and I ain't intending to give you more shit you can stir up about that damn bastard Artie Lee. Good riddance is what I say about it."

Raymond stands up.

"I think you've upset the old man enough for one day," he says. "Maybe it's time for you to get the hell out of here."

Maybe so, I concur, but that ought to be Eddie's call.

"It's our damn house," Raymond says, "and I say it's time to go."

I'm standing, wanting more than anything to punch Raymond Shaw, when the old man clears his throat.

"If it wasn't for that girl," he says, "we'd of got the whole damn bunch of 'em. They blackmailed us."

I ask him what girl.

He just shakes his head and says he's "done said enough."

On the way out, I hear Eddie trying to get out of that not-so-easy chair.

"Why don't you ask your damn momma about it," he calls after me. "She might tell you something. Maybe more than you want to know."

His laughter follows me as Raymond ushers me out.

We step out on the front porch.

Raymond moves a little too far into my personal space.

"You know," he says, "you shouldn't ought to be giving my daddy such a hard time. I don't appreciate it."

I tell him that I don't appreciate a lot of shit, but that sometimes you just have to live with life's little irritations.

He follows me out to the street, again way too close.

I turn.

"Razor," I tell him, "we're out here on a public street now. If you were just dying to kick my ass, this'd probably be a good place to do it. Otherwise, you ought to get out of my face.

"And one other thing: I'm glad David Shiflett's ass fried in that fire."

Hell, he's sixty-three and I'm pushing fifty-eight. How much damage could we do to each other? Oregon Hill roughnecks: the Seniors Tour.

He looks up at me, clenching and unclenching his fists.

"Maybe later," he says. Then he turns and walks back inside.

I've calmed down a little by the time I get back to Peggy's place. Awesome Dude is in the backyard, trying to chip away what's left of the ice from our recent storm off the steps. He doesn't seem to be making much progress.

My mother's pupils are only slightly dilated, so perhaps we can have a meaningful chat.

"What's this I hear about you not wanting me to do any more digging about Artie Lee?"

She sighs.

"I guess you've been talking to Andi."

"Yeah. I pretty much have to talk to one of you to find out what the other one's got on her mind."

Peggy offers me some coffee, and I accept. She fiddles with the Keurig we gave her for Christmas. When she gets it going at last, she turns to me.

"Well, you know I don't like it. Why do you want to know all this stuff? You never were that interested before."

I reply that I'd never been encouraged to be interested before. As a matter of fact, I was pretty much discouraged.

"Do you know I never even had a picture of the two of you?" I ask.

"I didn't have any pictures of him. I think my parents burned any I might have had."

I reach for my billfold.

"Arkie Bright had one," I tell her.

"Who?"

"Archangel Bright. He gave me this."

I hand her the picture of the two of them, taken before he got her pregnant with me.

"Arkie Bright," she says. "Damn, I hadn't heard that name in some time."

She looks at the picture, holding it close to her face.

"He was a handsome man," she says. "And, my God, how he could play that saxophone."

She hands the picture back to me.

"But that's old history," she says. "Water over the damn bridge or whatever."

I give her a rundown of what I've found out so far, including what Eddie Shaw said about his "trouble-making" tendencies.

"You talked to Eddie Shaw?"

"He's only about four blocks from here right now, down at his son's house."

"Eddie Shaw is nothing but trouble," she says. "You can't believe anything he says."

I ask Peggy what she knows about any trouble Artie Lee might have had with the authorities. I tell her that a source of mine thinks he might have somehow been involved in a bombing at a rally the year before he died.

"That's ridiculous," she says. "Artie, he didn't take any crap from anybody. That's one thing I loved about him. But he didn't have nothing to do with any damn Klan bombing."

I can't help but notice how she kind of stumbles over the word "love," like it's painful to her.

"I didn't say anything about it being a Klan rally."

She steps back.

"Well, I knew what you meant. You're just trying to trip me up now, like some damn lawyer."

We both sit at the table, sipping our coffee.

After what for us is a fairly long silence, she reaches across and takes my hand, an unusually tender gesture for my calloused old mom.

"Son," she says, "this is all too painful for me. I wish you would just let this whole thing die. It ain't worth it, believe me."

I don't make any promises, other than not making Artie Lee my life's work.

I didn't ask for this to fall into my lap, I remind her. If Philomena hadn't put the onus on me to take over the grave duties at Evergreen, I never would have gotten drawn into this.

Awesome Dude comes in. It appears that he's been scraping the back steps with the windshield scraper from the car. I make a note to buy my mother a snow shovel.

On the way out, I ask her one other thing.

"Eddie Shaw mentioned something about a girl. I think he said something about the cops being black-mailed over some girl, and that's what kept them from making a bunch of arrests after the bombing. You know anything about any of that?"

Peggy seems genuinely ignorant about this.

"Let it go, Willie," is her valedictory remark.

As much as I hate to bring up painful memories for my old mom, letting it go is not an option at this point.

—⁓—

TODAY IN Richmond History continues to be a real crowd-pleaser, according to the numbers our online geniuses produce. It's slightly behind the daily weather report and far in front of anything fossils like me would consider real news.

It's a quandary. If I keep my Number One ranking, B.S. will just want more and more of the same. If I intentionally or accidentally fuck it up, I move to the top of the layoff hit list.

I ran into a senior citizen two days ago at the new Buddy's over in the Devil's Triangle. He taught me what was then called journalism about a thousand years ago at VCU. I introduced myself and told him I'd been one of his students.

The guy must be at least eighty. He squinted up at me over his rail bourbon.

"They tell me you're the son of a bitch that does that Richmond history crap," he said. "What the hell are you all doing down there? You're supposed to be a damn newspaper. Don't you have any news to cover?"

I do some other things at the paper, I told him.

"Do me a favor," he said. "Don't tell anybody else you learned newspapering from me."

Then he turned back to his drink.

The one for tomorrow's a pip. On a January14th in the mid-fifties, a high school basketball game between two of the city schools had to be cut short because a player's father jumped one of the referees when he was running downcourt, trailing the play. The ref had just called the fifth foul on the son, and Dad didn't take it well.

They took the father to jail and the official to the hospital with a broken nose. I liked the arrestee's quote:

"I just thought the ref was unfair to our boys, cheating us like that. I thought he set a bad example."

And, no, I didn't have to make that one up.

CHAPTER FIFTEEN

Sunday

The back table at Joe's is packed. Goat Johnson made good on his promise and is in town trying to shake down some of his college's alums, making sure they remember alma mater in their wills. His wife, a lovely woman with obviously bad taste, is there, along with R.P. and his latest boy toy, plus Andy, Abe, Cindy, and me.

I'm wedged in the corner, wishing smoking was allowed. Goat, now going by Francis Xavier Johnson and far removed from his wayward Oregon Hill youth, says the school he is guiding is thinking about naming a building after him. Andy suggests something related to the English department, since Goat obviously had to engage in some creative résumé writing to con the academic world into giving him a job. I suggest chemistry in honor of our old friend's groundbreaking experiments with various recreational drugs.

"Just because you all decided to be broke-dicks your entire adult lives," Goat replies, "doesn't mean that everybody did."

Goat's wife, who seems to have sprung from higher up the evolutionary tree than our Oregon Hill gang, kind of flinches at "broke-dick." I guess Francis X.

doesn't engage in such gutter talk when he's wooing the old grads.

R.P. suggests that his employers might be amused if we sent them some photos from the old days, so they could appreciate how far he's come.

"I'm thinking maybe St. Patrick's Day, I believe it was 1976," he says. "You looked very fetching painted green, in your underpants."

Yeah, I agree, that was a St. Paddy's parade to remember.

"You didn't," Mrs. Johnson says.

Goat only laughs. He knows, or at least he's pretty sure, that we wouldn't scorch his glistening academic career over past indiscretions.

We do a toast to our missing member, Sammy Samms, the only one of us six who didn't make it to full adulthood. He wasn't any crazier than the rest of us. He was just unlucky.

Andy brings Goat up to speed regarding my quest to find out more about my father. We aren't awkward with each other about racial identity or any such bullshit, but it occurs to me that we never really talked about my missing dad. Lots of Hill kids had missing dads.

"Well," Goat says, "I wish you luck. I did one of those Ancestry.com DNA things and found out I'm about 25 percent Native American. Don't know where that came from."

Custalow suggests that maybe they're cousins.

"Hey, great," Goat says. "Maybe I can get in on that casino deal if I'm one-quarter Native American."

"Wrong tribe," Abe says. "That's the Pamunkeys."

Abe is a proud member of the Mattaponi nation, which has yet to be as fortunate as the Pamunkeys, who have received the Bureau of Indian Affairs license to get back through legalized gambling some of what was stolen from them long ago.

"Well," our academic star says, "tell me if you all get the green light. I can do Mattaponi."

I tell Goat that ancient history isn't really high on my list. I'm just trying to climb one branch up the family tree.

"Where the hell is Evergreen Cemetery anyhow?" Goat asks. "I never heard of it."

I explain that he likely wouldn't have, growing up in a place where Abe, his mother, and I were about the only ones giving the whitest place on Earth a little color.

We bullshit through another round of Bloody Marys, and then Goat and Mrs. Goat have a plane to catch, so the party breaks up, no doubt to the relief of our overworked waitress and those seated nearby.

"Where to?" Cindy asks. I tell her I've got a couple of places to go.

"If I didn't know better, Mr. Sneaky," she says, "I'd think you had a hot date somewhere."

I think she's kidding, but I invite her to come along.

"We're going to a cemetery," I tell her. "And then we're going to see Archangel Bright."

"Oh, the one whose son we went to see. The one you talked to the other day. Sounds like fun."

"We'll see."

Cindy hasn't been to the cemetery yet. She always seems to be somewhere else when I've gone there, or maybe I haven't been too encouraging. It is hard for me to understand how anyone could really give a damn about somebody else's family. These people who go on and on about how Robert E. Lee is their sixth cousin five times removed make me want to set the couch on fire just to create a diversion.

"You forget," Cindy says, "that this is my family too. We're in this together."

"Warts and all?"

"Till death do us part, or until your snoring gets worse."

My first wife, Jeanette, was like that, until I crapped all over her and torched our marriage. The next two Ms. Blacks, not so much. Maybe I haven't yet gotten used to having a spouse again who doesn't look on my family as a cross to bear.

Evergreen is as desolate as it was the last time I came. Here and there, someone has left flowers or some memento to brighten the dead gray of a January cemetery. About the only other color is the ivy choking the trees.

I open the trunk and take out the fake flowers I bought yesterday.

I lead Cindy down the hill to Artie Lee's grave. She seems much more fascinated than I am with the thousands of mostly forgotten souls buried here.

"How does this happen?" she asks as we stand among the ruins.

It was a business, I explain. When they filled the place up, I guess whoever was running things decided it was time to shut it down. We can see where some family members are keeping their late relatives' graves clear, and those AmeriCorps kids are doing their best, bless their hearts, but reclaiming Evergreen looks like a lost cause to me.

"All I'm here for," I tell Cindy, "is to take care of my one little corner."

My plan was to leave the faux flowers on Artie's grave. That's my sole purpose in being out here. Don't want it to be said that the Blacks don't take care of their dead. I'm freezing my ass off, but at least there are no weeds to pull up.

When we get there, though, I see that someone has beaten me to it. A flash of color leads me to Artie.

"I thought you said nobody was taking care of it," Cindy says.

The flowers that are already there are real, a couple of dozen red roses, although they look like they might be real dead pretty soon. Live flowers outdoors in January probably wasn't a great idea. They are sitting in some kind of container that's been planted into the earth next to the stone.

"I don't know," I tell her. "Maybe Richard Slade brought them." I'm pretty sure that isn't the case, since he's spending most of his waking hours doing the death watch over his mother. That's my best guess though. I don't have any others.

I bought some kind of cheap holder to put my cheesy permanent flowers in. I set it beside the real ones.

"That's nice," Cindy says as she sweeps away a few specks of dirt from the top of the stone.

At least there isn't much likelihood that some punks will steal the flowers. This place is too damn far away from civilization to entice the petty criminal element.

Cindy wants to wander around a bit. She says she intends to come out and volunteer to help clean the place up. I disengage a brier from my pants leg and tell her I'm sure they'll be happy to have all the help they can get.

"Tell me something about your father," she implores when we get back inside the car and turn the heater on. "I mean, he sounds like he led an interesting life."

"You might say that."

I've shown her the picture Arkie Bright gave me of my father and mother, and the one I made a copy of with my iPhone camera, and I've passed on the stories the other two Triple-A boys told me about his saxophone shenanigans with the Moonlights. Obviously, she wants to know more. Hell, so I do.

I tell her that I hope our next stop will shed more light on Artie Lee, for better or for worse.

—∾—

It's FIFTEEN to Arkie Bright's house. I'm not sure he'll be here. It's Sunday, so he might be terrorizing other motorists on I-95.

When we pull up, though, I see his car's out front, the same rusted-out Chevy I saw the other day.

I'm afraid Arkie is going to get tired of my ass on his front stoop. A less meddlesome person would wait a few days before returning, but this thing is gnawing at me. I've brought a six-pack this time, bought from the convenience store down the street from Arkie's place. Everybody else in the joint seemed to be buying lottery tickets or loitering and asking for spare change.

"This place looks worse than the Hill did when we were growing up," Cindy says. I can't deny that. Young bloods, maybe drinking beer with spare change from the convenience store, are hanging out where I saw them the other day.

I lock the car and lead Cindy up the steps to Arkie Bright's front door.

His face does not brighten when he sees me. I explain that I was just in the neighborhood and thought I'd say hello. When the six-pack comes into view, he opens the door wide enough for us to come in.

He offers us a couple of the beers I brought. Cindy and I both demur.

"Well," he says, "I'm gonna have one."

He limps into the kitchen and puts five of them in the fridge, then comes back with the sixth can open in his hand.

He's very cordial to Cindy, as most people are when they meet her. She has that effect. I think it's the smile, wide and genuine. I told her once that bringing her along on difficult interviews with uncooperative subjects might be a good idea.

"You know," I said, "like when college boys bring a Labrador retriever to the beach so the girls will talk to them."

She did not seem to appreciate the analogy.

To make conversation, I tell Arkie I'm surprised he's not in Fredericksburg today, visiting his sister.

"Aw, man," he says, setting his beer down on the coffee table, "it's a long story."

It isn't that long, but it's kind of sad. The state has just decided to crack down on speeders by making everybody who isn't breaking the sound barrier move out of the fast lane on the interstates. Nobody told Arkie apparently. He got a ticket last Sunday for not going fast enough in the left lane of I-95.

"Sonsabitches was flashing their lights at me," he grumbles, "like they own the damn road. They was lucky I ain't packing heat anymore."

Eventually, one of the cars behind Arkie belonged to a state trooper, who pulled him over and wrote him up for, I guess, a non-speeding ticket.

"After that mess, I just didn't feel like making the trip this week," he says. He looks defeated.

Maybe, I suggest, US 1, which runs alongside 95, might be a good alternative.

"Yeah," he says, "I might ought to do that."

We eventually get around to Topic A: Artie Lee.

I clear my throat.

"There's a retired cop I know. He was the investigating officer in that Klan bombing back in 1960. He said something that made me pretty sure that my father was involved in all that somehow."

I lean closer.

"He said something about a girl. He said something like, if it hadn't been for that damn girl, a bunch of people would have been in deep trouble. Something about blackmail."

Arkie takes a sip.

"I don't know nothing about no girl," he says. "I don't know nothing about that."

"The cop's name is Eddie Shaw."

Arkie looks at me.

"Hadn't heard that name in a while," he says, so quiet I can barely hear him.

"So you remember him?"

"Oh, man. Him and his partner, they was the worst. They were on everybody's asses—excuse me, ma'am—about that bombing. They kept telling us they were going to send us all to the chair."

Arkie says that after the bombing, the police were always stopping black drivers on the highway for little or no reason.

"They wanted somebody to talk, and that Shaw cracker, he told me one time when he pulled me for a busted taillight, which he busted his own self, that if somebody didn't start talking, they'd find a way to make us talk. He said the first one that talked might get a break, but God help the others."

"So who were they after?"

He looks at me.

"Who the hell do you think?"

"Artie Lee?"

It's so obvious that he doesn't even answer.

"But why? Did they think he did the bombing?"

Arkie Bright gets up from his chair. He's so agitated that I'm afraid he's going to have a stroke or something.

"You're asking too many questions, son," he says, waving his bony index finger at me. "We took care of that mess back then. We did what we had to do. Cut our losses, know what I mean?"

"What about the girl? That girl Eddie Shaw mentioned."

Arkie is moving around the room, looking everywhere but at me.

"There's one person that can tell you about that girl," he says at last, "and that's Arthur Meeks. But when you talk to him, you don't tell him I sent you."

Since Arthur Meeks is the one who put me on to Arkie, I tell him, this seems kind of fruitless.

Arkie comes back and eases himself gingerly into his chair.

"Arthur is the one that made it happen," he says. "But you're going to have to get it from him. He can tell you about that girl, if he wants to."

There's one more thing I need to ask before I leave Arkie Bright, maybe for the last time.

"Eddie Shaw said something about asking my mother about it."

Arkie shakes his head.

"Aw, son," he says, "you're gettin' in way over your head now. Just let stuff be."

He points toward the door with his cane.

"Now," he says, "I'm going to have to ask you all to leave. Don't want to be rude, but I ain't got anything else to say about that mess."

Letting stuff be isn't in my DNA. Peggy could have told Arkie Bright that. But I've gotten about all I'm going to get from him. I leave him alone to finish the rest of his six-pack.

"Wow," Cindy says when we're in the car headed back across the bridge, "is he saying your father might have been involved in killing a couple of people?"

I tell her I'm still not straight on that, but I do plan to pay another visit to Arthur Meeks tomorrow.

She looks over at me.

"You don't plan to let this go, do you?"

"You were the one who wanted to know more about my father, remember?"

When I check my cell phone, which I've apparently had on mute for the last few hours, I see that Sally Velez has called.

Shit. The goddamn Morgue Report.

Maybe I should tie a string around my finger.

So I drop Cindy off at the Prestwould and head into the office to either find or manufacture a compelling blast from the past.

Arkie Bright has my head spinning. As much as I like to go after a good story, I'm starting to feel like this one might be too good for my own good.

CHAPTER SIXTEEN

Monday

The latest Morgue Report, cobbled together sometime after six last night, has the advantage of being verbatim true. A nor'easter on a January 16th in the early thirties eroded the front yard of some rich guy's Rappahannock River house so badly that the porch became one with the river, with the rest of the place sure to follow.

The owner, who had sense enough to get out before his castle did a swan dive into the Rapp, said two previous storms had eaten most of the river bank away, "But I didn't think it would happen again."

Optimism, in my experience, is a fool's bet.

I stayed and did one for Tuesday too. When I filed that one, Sally gave me a very insincere standing ovation. I told her that if editors didn't have to nag, there'd be no use for them whatsoever.

When I got back to the Prestwould, Cindy was not in the best of spirits.

It seems that the Chipster, making one final bid to separate his mother from her life savings, called while I was gone.

"He said this was his last chance to make something of himself," she said.

I noted that he was pretty young to be down to his last chance, and that Cindy's ex, while temporarily cash-poor, would no doubt bob back to the top soon and be able to help their son in his bid to become a restaurateur. I think "shit floats" was the phrase I used.

"I know," she said, twice.

I asked her if she had turned him down again.

"I said I'd think about it."

Good God. I bit hard on my tongue and didn't say that she might as well go ahead and write him a check now. Or just take the money and throw it out the sixth-floor window. The bums would be happy at least. There is no use whatsoever in telling any woman that her only offspring is a worthless asshole who will turn her dollars into nickels. The bistro or brasserie or whatever the hell kind of culinary money pit Chip Marshman has in mind has about the same chance as that house on the Rappahannock.

Cindy sensed my disapproval.

"Well, what am I supposed to do? He's my son, for Christ's sake."

I eased my toes into the piranha-rich waters of mother-son affairs and suggested again that maybe Donnie Marshman ought to be the one backing his son.

"After all," I said, "he's not having to write alimony checks anymore."

None of this seemed to sway Cindy, who would not commit beyond a tepid, "Maybe you're right."

"Have you talked to him about it?"

She gave me what might be described as a hard look.

"Donnie? Hell, no. I'd rather pull out my fingernails with a set of pliers than talk to that piece of crap."

Her reaction reinforced what I already knew: Don't get on a Hill girl's shit list.

—⚬—

TODAY, ON my day off, I leave home not long after Cindy. She's back to the educational salt mines now that our latest snow has melted enough so that tomorrow's leaders can safely ride school buses.

I edge my way out the front door, keeping Butterball back with my trailing foot. She doesn't want to go to work with daddy. She wants me to feed her, as she hasn't had nourishment in more than an hour.

Custalow is downstairs, trying to get a stain out of the Oriental carpet in the lobby, the work of some hound's overactive bladder and his lazy-ass owner's decision to take Rover through the lobby instead of using the basement alley entrance.

"What did you find out yesterday?" he asks when I stop to commiserate with him. Abe wasn't in until late last night, seeing Stella Stellar off on the next leg of her big-break tour.

I tell him what Arkie Bright said.

"Man," he says, "this just gets deeper and deeper, doesn't it? I mean, you think your dad could have been involved in something like that? And it had something to do with the wreck?"

I tell Abe that anything is possible at this point. I'm starting to get a picture here, and it's kind of making the hairs on my arms stand up. Mum is the word, though, until I get more information.

"So you're going to see that other guy, Meems?"

"Meeks. Yeah. But first I've got to check in on Philomena."

While we're talking, Feldman comes up. McGrumpy is getting ready to blow a gasket about inconsiderate pet owners, how we never should have let dogs in the Prestwould to start with, how he fought it all along, blah-blah-blah, when I cut him off.

"Mr. Feldman," I ask, frowning and pointing to the stain, which looks eerily like a map of the commonwealth, "did you do that?"

—⟋⟍—

PHILOMENA IS no better, and nobody expects her to be.

Chanelle, who's taking half a day off work to be with Richard, says the doctors tell them it's only a matter of time. At least Philomena looks peaceful.

Richard's there, too, sleeping in the most comfortable chair in this cramped room. He looks like he's lost ten pounds since his mother came in here. I feel for him. Like me, he is the only child of a single parent. He and Philomena have been through a lot. I'm just glad he had a few years after he was exonerated to spend with the only person who believed he was innocent. But that's comfort as cold as the January weather outside.

While Chanelle and I chat, he wakes up and apologizes for sleeping. Everybody, I tell him, needs at least a couple of hours of sleep a day.

"Aw," he says, "it isn't so bad. I can doze off half an hour or so at a time. Could do more, but there's always somebody coming in here checking on her, like they can do any good now."

Yeah, the folks here are basically waiting for her bed to free up at this point, but they still come knocking on a regular basis. Maybe they bill you by how many times they stop by.

With all his troubles, Richard thinks to ask me about my quest for Artie Lee.

I tell him about what I've learned from Arkie Bright, and that I have been directed back to Arthur Meeks.

"He wasn't too eager to talk much the last time I saw him."

Richard shakes his head.

"I don't know what the problem is. I saw his son the other day, and he said something about some reporter nosing around there. I guess that was you. Said it made the old man kind of nervous."

If Arthur Meeks knows what I suspect he does, he has reason to be nervous. As bad as I hate hounding the old guy again, there doesn't seem to be any other way to get where I'm going.

If knowledge is power, I'm a little better armed for this meeting with Arthur Meeks than I was last time.

—〰—

When I get to the Meeks residence in Sandston, I see that there's a light on in the living room, despite the fact that it's eleven in the morning. It's cold as a bitch. As I knock, a plane coming into Richmond International flies over low enough to make me duck by reflex. I guess Arthur Meeks is glad the former Richard Evelyn Byrd Flying Field doesn't have more business than it does.

Meeks comes to the door about the time I'm starting to lose feeling in my fingers. We pretty much go through the same conversation as before. He finally lets me in on the strength of being Artie Lee's son, but I wonder if he remembers our last visit. Recalling what Richard Slade said about Arthur being uneasy over our last contact, though, I'm pretty damn sure he hasn't forgotten me.

"So, young man," he says after he turns down the volume on the TV from deafening to a whisper and limps his way back to his favorite chair, "what brings you out here? Not a good day to be out and about."

No, I agree, it's not.

"But there's still some things I need to find out, about Artie Lee."

He frowns.

"I thought maybe I hadn't seen the last of you," he says.

I go through what I've learned since the last time we talked. I tell him what Arkie Bright told me, and what an "informed source" high in the police department said. When I tell him about my meeting with Eddie Shaw, he has pretty much the same reaction as Arkie did.

He looks like he wants to spit but swallows it instead.

"I remember that one," he says. "Yeah. I'd hoped he'd be dead by now."

"Mr. Meeks," I say, leaning forward in the straight-backed chair, "I know about the Klan bombing, and I'm pretty sure my father had something to do with it."

I don't know if I'm glad or sad when he doesn't deny it.

Arthur Meeks doesn't believe in linear. He goes off on a long, wide tangent that I am hopeful will eventually zero in on that elusive bastard, the truth.

"Artie was an angry young man," he says. "I reckon we all were. But Artie, he tended to act on things."

He tells me about the time my father, when he was "not more than twelve, I don't suppose," was hired by a white man to help him sell watermelons.

Artie's job was to sit in the bed of the truck while the farmer drove through black neighborhoods, hawking the melons piled up back there. Artie was supposed to haul the melons off and collect the money.

"This fella," Meeks says, "was kind of cheap. I'd done that same job for him and thought he cheated me. So I wouldn't go with him again. But Artie needed the money, I guess."

They worked all day, Meeks says, and Artie told him later they must have sold a hundred melons. Artie Lee was supposed to get two dollars.

"But when they got through, the man counted the melons and said they were short, that Artie must have slipped a few to his friends.

"Well, that was a damn lie. Artie Lee was a lot of things, but he didn't lie and he didn't steal."

So the farmer only gave him one dollar and warned him about stealing from him.

"There wasn't nothin' Artie could do about it, or at least it seemed that way. But he found a way. He told me about it after he did it."

Two nights later, Artie Lee, who knew where the farmer's watermelon patch was, went over in the middle of the night and busted up as many of the man's melons as he could with a sledgehammer.

"That farmer, he had to know Artie Lee did it," Arthur Meeks says, laughing at the nearly seventy-year-old memory. "But there wasn't much he could do about it except cuss."

Meeks looks at me.

"That's the way he was. Didn't take no shit off nobody, no matter what the consequences."

He dropped out of school in the middle of his senior year, Meeks says, after the furnace in the black high school died and the kids had to sit in classrooms "that wasn't much warmer than it was outside."

Meeks says he tried to get Artie to stay on the rest of the year "but he said, 'Hell no.' If the state of Virginia didn't think enough of him to put heat in the classrooms, he didn't think enough of it to keep on going to their damn school."

The old man shakes his head.

"It was just the way he was. He'd do things that hurt him, just to make a point about something. He went back and finished up the next year, after they fixed the furnace."

I feel in my bones that we're getting to what Arthur Meeks has probably wanted to tell somebody since 1961. A few uh-huhs and head nods are all I need to contribute to keep the story moving forward.

"What really set him off, though, was the Klan."

The big rally over Fourth of July weekend in 1960 was announced weeks in advance. Artie Lee, who was working with a highway construction crew when he wasn't traveling with the Moonlighters, tried to get anybody he could to join him in making some kind of statement, without any luck.

"He just wanted them to know that we wouldn't take that kind of shit," Meeks says.

The old man sits back for a minute. He seems like he's short of breath.

"You got to give me a minute," he says, between wheezes. "The doctor says I shouldn't get too excited."

Great. Am I going to kill this old man just to find out what happened a lifetime ago?

He gets his second wind though.

"I know I shouldn't be telling you all this," he says, the sweetest words a decent reporter can ever hope to hear. "But somebody's got to hear it. I ain't even told my son. And, hell, Artie Lee's dead. I don't reckon there's much they can do to me at this point either.

"And that Shaw guy, that cop? Well, he can go to jail or to hell, I don't give a damn which."

A week before the rally, Artie Lee told his two best friends what he had in mind.

"Arkie, he said he didn't want to hear nothin' more about it, said to leave him out of it, just pretend he wasn't even there. But I stayed and listened. I might have tried to talk him out of it, but to tell you the truth, I was about as pissed off as Artie Lee was.

"He had my blessing."

The old man stops to blow his nose.

"The thing is, wasn't nobody supposed to get hurt."

My father had learned enough about explosives, working with that construction crew, and he had managed to get his hands on a few sticks of dynamite.

A man who worked with him on the road crew had done time in prison for blowing up a neighbor's unoccupied house over some disagreement, using a timer.

"I guess that's where Artie got the idea from. He got the guy to show him how to do it. He told me the fella wasn't told what he wanted to know for, and he didn't ask. He was black, too, so I don't reckon he was too upset after he heard about the bombing."

The night of the rally, Artie Lee hid in the edge of the woods, in a place no other black person wanted to be within ten miles of. When he saw a police car drive up, he thought he'd found the perfect place to plant the dynamite.

"He said the cop got out and walked over toward where they had the cross and all, maybe a hundred yards away. There was nobody else anywhere close by. So he put that dynamite with the timer under the car.

"He'd planned it to go off in an hour, about the time all them white bastards were in their glory, burning that cross."

Artie Lee wasn't around when the dynamite blew. He walked through the woods to where he'd parked off a rut road, and he left.

"He said he didn't know anything about it until the next morning, when he saw it in the paper. He figured there'd be something in there about them Klansmen getting a little of their own medicine, but then he sees that there's two people dead."

The cop probably was supposed to meet his honey there and go back with her to his car. And they were comfortably entwined in the back seat when Artie Lee's bomb went off.

There was hell to pay over the following weeks and months, Arthur Meeks says. Nobody black was immune to the harassment as the city, state, and county police tried to avenge the killing of one of their own.

"There wasn't much said about why a city policeman was at a Ku Klux Klan rally in the first place. All that mattered was that he was dead, and they were damn sure one of us black folks did it."

It took the cops until the next spring to get a tip about a highway crew that had somehow lost a few sticks of dynamite the summer before. It didn't take them much longer to discover that a black ex-con who knew how to blow shit up was on that crew.

"And it didn't take them long to squeeze information out of that fella, that he'd showed one of his fellow workers how to make a bomb."

The ex-con called Artie Lee, who was working in a lumberyard by that time, to tell him the police were soon going to be on him like white on rice. And Artie Lee disappeared.

"So they come after me and Arkie Bright."

They knew that the three of them were thick as thieves, and they figured Arthur and Arkie must be in on the bombing.

"They told us that they knew we'd planned it together, which was a lie. That bastard Shaw, he said they'd find somebody who would finger all three of us. We knew he couldn't do that without gettin' somebody to lie, but he wasn't above that."

Arthur Meeks is looking straight ahead. I'm not sure he's even aware I'm in the room anymore. Maybe he's had this same conversation with himself more than once over the decades.

"They had us by the short hairs. They told us we were going to either fry or spend the rest of our lives in prison, but that they might be convinced that we were innocent bystanders if we just told them Artie Lee did it and told them where he was."

"So, did you do it?"

The old man blinks.

"Well, it wasn't quite as simple as that."

And then he tells me, or tells the wall in front of him, about the deal he made with the devil.

CHAPTER SEVENTEEN

Tuesday

The call comes while I'm having my morning coffee. Butterball is in my lap, trying to cover my pants with cat hair.

Raymond Shaw gets right to the point.

"We need to talk."

When I ask about what, he says, "You know god-damn well what."

I have a pretty good idea. Last Saturday's conversation seems to have lit a fire under Razor's old man. Perhaps Eddie Shaw doesn't want to spend what's left of his sorry-ass life in prison. I still don't know all the details, but Eddie is in deep enough shit that he's reaching out to a guy I'm pretty sure he never wanted to talk to again.

I ask Raymond where.

"Why not come back over to my place?"

This doesn't work for me. When I was feeling out Eddie Shaw about my father's death, the house on Pine Street seemed safe enough. Now that Eddie and Raymond and maybe a few of their kin have an idea where this is going, a neutral site seems like a better idea. The memory of Eddie's nephew, David Junior Shiflett, luring me into a trap and almost killing me a few years ago hasn't quite left my memory bank.

"I'll meet you down by the overlook, at the benches there," I tell Razor.

"It's cold as a bitch," he complains.

It isn't cold enough, I'm thinking, to put my ass inside Raymond Shaw's house again, not with what I know and what they suspect I know. I've developed a fondness for wide-open spaces.

So, despite Raymond's whining about his old man's health, we agree to meet at the overlook. Hell, it's going to be almost fifty today. The snow's melted.

The meeting's set for eleven. I've written my Morgue Report piece for tomorrow already, so there's nothing much to do for the next hour and a half except watch the end of an old John Garfield movie, brush off cat hair, and then go find Custalow.

He's down in the basement. The boiler, held together by spit and duct tape, is acting up again.

"Want to take a little trip with me?" I ask him.

It seems to me that the substantial presence of Abe Custalow might make the Shaws and whoever else comes along even less likely to go all homicidal on me.

Abe says he'll have to check with Marcia the manager, but he thinks he can get away for a couple of hours "if I can get this damn thing fixed."

He bangs the side of the boiler with a wrench, which doesn't seem to help.

He doesn't ask me to explain, but I do anyhow. I don't want Abe walking into an Oregon Hill shit show without prior warning.

"And that's what the old man, that Meeks fella, told you? Damn, Willie, that's some heavy stuff. Do you think they suspect that you've been talking to Meeks?"

I tell him I don't see how, but that they're obviously spooked enough to try to work something out.

"This oughta be good," Abe says. "I never did like that son of a bitch Razor."

I don't think Razor Shaw and his cronies ever picked on Custalow when we were boys. I say that because they stopped messing with me when Abe became my best friend. Even as a younger kid, he wasn't somebody sane people went out of their way to harass.

Abe gets the blessing of Marcia. I promise to have him back by twelve thirty, a promise I hope I can keep.

On the short drive over, I ask Abe about Stella Stellar and her pursuit of fame and fortune.

"Oh, she said it wasn't as great as she'd hoped," he says. "I talked to her on the phone yesterday. She said they played at a club in Columbia, South Carolina, where there were more waiters than customers."

He says she's also come to the realization that she isn't really all that fond of her fellow band members, all of whom are guys.

"She said it was OK jamming with them and doing gigs at clubs around here, where they could go back to their own beds at night, but that some of them seem to think that part of going on the road is getting fucked up. And she says they don't play especially well, or even remember all the words, when they're fucked up."

He chuckles.

"She says she kind of knew that all guys were assholes, but she never had positive proof before."

Abe says they're going to be on the road for a week longer, then come back here for a couple of days, then hit the road again, "so I guess I'll be imposing on your and Cindy's hospitality for a little longer."

I assure him it's never an imposition. As usual, we never talk about his late son or my part in that lateness.

We drive through the skinny streets of the Hill. They used to be wider, in my memory. I think they've shrunk because everybody has these fat-ass vehicles now. Sometimes it's hard to squeeze past them on the one-way streets when two of them are parked side-by-side. They're so damn big they blot out the sun.

When we come out at the overlook, the sun breaks through. Behind us are the newer condos that blend with the rest of Oregon Hill like pearls on a bag lady. In front of us and below is the James. It's roaring today, full of melted mountain snow headed east. The rocks glint in the sun like jewels. As soon as the temperature rises ten degrees more, suicidal kayakers will be dodging them, but today the river belongs to the egrets and even the occasional bald eagle. Belle Isle, splitting the waters, is probably human-free today, too, unless some of the homeless are really desperate.

The benches where I told Raymond Shaw to meet us are up ahead. And I see that same Crown Vic alongside the curb. I park my Honda behind it.

When Custalow and I get out, the car starts unloading. Razor and Eddie get out of the front seats. The two back doors open, and out step a pair of guys ugly enough to be related to the Shaws.

It's worse than that, I discover. Raymond informs me that they are Shifletts, also cousins of the late David Junior. Great.

"You might remember Abe Custalow," I say, turning to him. "He thought he'd come along for the ride."

"Oh, yeah," Eddie says, looking up and squinting in the sun, "you're the one that killed that fella."

Abe doesn't say anything. The two cousins' contribution to the conversation so far has consisted of scowls.

Raymond tries to get us to step inside the car, but I'm set on having this discussion in the great outdoors.

So we go to the benches. Eddie and the older of the cousins sit. The rest of us stand, facing them.

"We hear you been asking around," Raymond says, "about my dad and all that shit that happened way back when."

I'm not sure how deep Raymond's knowledge of my snooping goes. Maybe he's just guessing.

"What we want," the older cousin adds, "is for you to leave us the fuck alone. What's the old saying, let the dead bury the dead?"

I kneel and look Eddie straight in the eye.

"Just tell me what happened. Just tell me, and I promise you I won't ever use your name in the paper, or anywhere else."

I'm ready to go the not-for-attribution route to find out what happened to my father. These assholes probably don't know what a concession that is. It pains my ink-stained soul.

Eddie Shaw doesn't say anything for the longest time, and then he starts talking. His son and the cousin sitting beside him try to control him from time to time, but Eddie still does what Eddie wants to do, and he does still hold the deed to Raymond's house, so they have to take me at my word and let Eddie talk.

"Do you know what it looks like when somebody gets blown up with that much dynamite?" he asks, his voice rising a little. Even so, I have to lean forward and strain to hear him over the roar of the river below us. "They were in pieces, just blown to pieces. There wasn't no way we were going to let a bunch of niggers get away with that."

"So you got even."

He grins at me, his yellow teeth catching the sunlight.

"Somebody sure as hell did," he says.

"And I'll bet you're just the man who can tell me how 'somebody' did it."

"You think you know everything. You don't know shit."

So he tells me his version of how it all went down.

The cops found out about the ex-con, who led them to Artie Lee, but they couldn't find him for a couple of weeks.

"And then we got a tip," the old man says. "Or, rather, the fellas that did the deed got a tip."

They found out where Artie was hiding out. They waited for him to come out, and when he did, "they took care of business."

"So the wreck wasn't an accident? Is that what you're telling me?"

"There wasn't anybody to say different. When they examined the scene afterward, they found a Ten High bottle inside, almost empty. He just went off that curve pretty as you please, not even any skid marks. They figured he knew the jig was up, so to speak."

I look Eddie in the eye.

"But you knew that wasn't true."

Eddie Shaw laughs.

"Yeah, we knew a lot of shit. But the thing is, you don't have a lick of proof. That's why I'm telling you this. Your old man was a murderer, a damn assassin's what he was. And if somebody took care of his ass on that curve on Route 5, well, good for them. And good luck pinning it on anybody."

The old man sits back. He looks exhausted.

"That's why we wanted to talk," Raymond Shaw says. "We wanted you to know what happened. And we want you to stop bothering Eddie here. Let him have some peace."

So it's time to turn over my hole cards.

"I'd like to do that, Razor," I say and see him get all squinty-eyed when I throw that old nickname at him, "but I've found out some things that kind of fill in some blanks in the story. Do you want me to fill you in, Razor?"

And so I spend a few minutes telling Raymond and Eddie Shaw and their malevolent posse most of what Arthur Meeks told me.

They get kind of quiet.

Then Raymond takes two steps and stands over me as I kneel by his father. Abe moves a couple of steps forward himself, so that he's as close to Raymond as Raymond is to me. The two cousins seem ready to jump in, too, and I'm wondering if maybe I should've brought Andy and R.P. along, or at least a firearm.

"Whatever that old man told you," Raymond says, "you can't prove it."

"Maybe not," I tell him, "but I didn't tell you everything."

So I give them, as they say, the rest of the story. And then I reached into my coat pocket. The cousins move in, no doubt thinking from their criminal experience that I'm packing.

Then I pull out the document, the one Arthur Meeks gave me.

I hand it to Eddie Shaw. He reads it, his lips moving, and I watch his booze-flushed face turn as white as the sheet of paper he's holding.

CHAPTER EIGHTEEN

Arthur Meeks likes to save things. I should have known that when he showed me all those photographs he'd hoarded from his long life, or the forty years of *National Geographics*, piled up in his spare bedroom from floor to damn ceiling. So I had a hunch, but I found out for sure yesterday.

What he told me, and what he gave me, has made the Shaws and Shifletts a little nervous.

—m—

Meeks wasn't fond of spending the rest of his life in prison. He figured that even if he gave up Artie Lee, the cops might find a way to put his ass away too. And he couldn't even give them that.

"I couldn't tell 'em where Artie was," he told me, "because I didn't know myself."

He said he hoped he wouldn't have told them anyhow, but since he had already spilled his guts about the bombing, Arthur Meeks probably had gone into save-your-butt mode.

"They was going to take me and Arkie Bright away, even said they'd find a way to put my wife in prison for bein' a damn accomplice.

"I had to find a way to get 'em off my back."

What he found was Roseanna Rucker.

She was fourteen, Meeks said, but she could and did pass for eighteen on a regular basis.

And she had been raped.

She was a local girl, a distant cousin of Meeks. She lived in the same neighborhood. She had the good or bad fortune to be an early bloomer, a pretty girl who drew the attention of grown men who let their dicks override their moral compasses. She was light-skinned and already, at fourteen, built for action.

"She was a little wild," he said, "but she didn't mean no harm."

Meeks said he heard the story two days after it happened, from Roseanna's mother.

The girl came home one night in early April of 1961 with her dress torn and one of her shoes missing. She was prone to running off, sometimes not coming back for a day or two. Her mother, who had six other children, couldn't control her.

"She said two white policemen dragged her into a car, took her to the Lawry Motel and took turns with her."

Roseanna Rucker wasn't a virgin, by all accounts, but up until that time, the sex had been consensual.

"Plus," Meeks said, stating the obvious, "she wasn't but fourteen."

When Meeks talked with the girl and she described her rapists, he knew who she meant. The same two detectives had been hounding everyone with dark skin pigment ever since the bombing. Meeks said he supposed that they had come to think they could do any damn thing they wanted, up to and including the unspeakable.

"Her momma came to me because there wasn't no man in the house, and she didn't know what to do about it. Nobody was going to believe a black girl's word against no white policemen."

Meeks didn't know what to do either. He was already Number Two on the cops' shit list, behind Artie Lee himself.

But, with the figurative noose tightening around his neck, he thought he might be able to work a deal. It would involve using a teenage girl who already had been used grievously.

"I couldn't think of nothing else to do."

He got in touch with Arkie Bright and told him what his plan was.

"He didn't much want to go along with it, but I told him he was already in deep water, and this was going to be his life preserver. He finally saw the light."

Meeks knew the man who worked the front desk at the Lawry Motel. The man was white, "but he wasn't a bad sort."

He knew what was going on in Room 14. Roseanna wasn't the first girl the two detectives had taken there, either willingly or by force. It had been made clear to him that, if he knew what was good for him, he'd look the other way when one of the cops came in and demanded the key to "their" room.

"I talked to him, about Roseanna, and he didn't remember her, and I could tell he wasn't going to remember anything else, either, for his own good."

The front-desk guy wasn't exactly on the side of the detectives though. He just wanted whatever happened to happen without his greasy fingerprints on it.

Meeks had to go to Roseanna and get her to go along with his plan.

"I told her that they wouldn't bother her no more if she did what we asked her to do, and that maybe we could get back at them. And I promised the child that no harm would come to her, that we'd be there to protect her."

The two cops liked to eat at a hole-in-the wall diner near the motel. The plan was for Roseanna to hang around outside 'til they came out and play up to them, like she'd like a repeat performance.

"It was terrible, asking her to do that," Meeks said. "She was scared, but she was brave too. Bein' brave when you're scared, that's hard."

She made them swear to her that they would be there for her.

Two nights later, Meeks and Arkie Bright dropped the girl off a couple of hundred yards from the diner, and then they went back to the motel and waited in Arkie's car.

"It could have gone wrong six ways to Sunday," Meeks told me. "They could have just brushed her off, or got suspicious, or just took her out in the woods. But we knew they had a fondness for the Lawry."

Not more than forty-five minutes after they dropped Roseanna off, they saw the Richmond cop car come pulling into the gravel parking lot at the motel.

"We ducked down so they wouldn't see us. Then, when we saw the one, that Shaw bastard, go into the office and get the key, and we saw the other one lead the girl over to Room14, we waited half a minute, and then we went and got the other key."

The front-desk man acted like he didn't want to give it to them, but Meeks told him not to worry, that they'd tell the detectives that they'd followed the detectives there and forced him to give it up.

"Plus," he said, "I had my shotgun with me."

Arkie had a Polaroid camera with him.

Meeks said the cops might've acted differently if they hadn't been so guilty. When the door flew open, they already had the girl's blouse off and were in the process of removing their pants.

"I told them cops, if somebody goes for a gun, I'll blow their damn head off," he said, "and I guess they must of believed me."

Arkie got a couple of flash shots, and they retrieved the girl. Meeks told the cops that she was his cousin, and he knew they had raped her, and that they had best not ever try anything like that again.

"Felt good to have the whip hand for once."

They left with Roseanna before the cops could put their pants back on.

Five days later, Meeks got in touch with Shaw through a black cop he knew.

"Didn't tell him what it was about, just that we needed to talk."

They met inside the AME Zion church Meeks and his family went to.

"Figured he might not kill me in there."

Shaw brought the other detective with him. Meeks brought Arkie Bright.

Meeks explained how it was. If the police would back off on everybody except Artie Lee, they would back off on trying to get Shaw and his partner arrested for raping a fourteen-year-old girl. It wouldn't be that easy, Meeks figured, with the girl being black, but they did have a couple of pretty good photographs, and the girl was willing to say they had raped her once and made her go to the motel a second time.

"They called us every kind of nigger. But in the end, they knew they had to give it up. We assured them that there were other copies of those pictures, and that the girl was out of state, staying with relatives, which was a lie."

The two detectives and two-thirds of the Triple-A boys agreed to those terms.

"We wanted them to shake hands, but they wouldn't."

After that, in the dwindling time left in Artie Lee's short life, there was no more harassment of anyone in the black community.

"I didn't know if they would of kept their word forever or not," Meeks said, "and I didn't know if we could of made that rape charge stick, considering when and where we was, but I reckon all parties concerned figured it was a fair deal."

When Arthur Meeks had finished his story, I said I guessed everybody came out OK except for Artie Lee.

Meeks looked at me with his bloodshot eyes. I thought he might cry.

"I got to tell you, we felt bad about that. He was our friend. But Artie was gone, man. There wasn't any way he wasn't going down for what he did."

I didn't want to agree, but I saw his point. Cut your losses.

But there was one more thing I had to ask.

"If you didn't know where Artie Lee was, who did? I mean, who told them? Or did they just get lucky in finding him the night he was killed?"

Arthur Meeks shook his head.

"If I knew, I'd tell you. We was hoping he had gone out of state, out of the country, Mars, somewhere where they couldn't get him. But then we heard the news, and we knew, right then, that it wasn't no accident."

I asked him what became of the girl.

"She's still living out there, not a mile from where we grew up. She's a deaconess in the church now."

Just to add a little insurance, in case the detectives decided to go back on their deal, Meeks did one more thing.

He took Roseanna Rucker to his minister, who also happened to be a notary public. He had the girl write down exactly what the detectives did to her, chapter and verse, and the preacher notarized it. Then they had the preacher notarize what Meeks and Arkie Bright wrote, testifying to what they saw that night in Room 14.

"The preacher was kind of taken aback. I think he wanted to pray with us, but I told him we'd worry about the Lord later.

"Kept them with me all this time," he told me, handing me the two documents. "Didn't know if I'd ever need 'em or not, but if it'll help you, you're welcome to them."

—m—

So I made copies and returned the originals to Meeks. And that's what Eddie Shaw and his son and cousins have just finished reading.

"This is bullshit," Raymond said when he'd finally finished. Eddie didn't say anything, just sat there staring out across the river at Belle Isle.

Might be, I conceded, but I'm betting not.

I kneel again, so I'm eye-to-eye with Eddie.

"I don't want anything from you but the truth," I tell him. "Your name isn't going to go in the paper, like I promised, but if you don't tell me who killed my father and how, the chief is going to get a copy of this, and we can go from there."

Raymond looks like he'd like to kick my ass all the way down to the river, but Custalow puts a hand on his shoulder, which seems to calm him a bit.

The old man looks rattled.

"I need to think," he says at last, so soft I have to ask him to repeat it.

And so we leave it at that. I tell Eddie to not take too much time.

In the car, Custalow says, "Holy shit. You think that old bastard did it?"

I lit a Camel.

"I just want to hear him say it."

I drop Abe off at the Prestwould with fifteen minutes to spare and head upstairs to feed Butterball. Custalow claps me on the shoulder as we part, him for the basement and me for the sixth floor.

"I just wish one of those peckerheads had made some kind of a move," he says. "It's been a long time since I've kicked the shit out of a Shaw or a Shiflett."

CHAPTER NINETEEN

Wednesday

Last night was quiet enough. I got one ahead on the Morgue Report with a fascinating story from the mid-fifties about a preservationist, of which our fair city has more than its share, going down with her house, so to speak.

She was trying to save some shack on the South Side that had alleged historical significance, like Patrick Henry took a crap there or something. The city, which is not inclined to tear down anything, had condemned it.

So she decided to squat in the shack, like those idiots who climb trees so they won't be cut down. Except she didn't tell anybody, just broke in one night, planning to make a big fuss in the morning, when the demolition was scheduled to take place.

But she lit a candle and fell asleep, and the shack caught fire. Good night, old house. Good night, preservation lady.

I felt bad for the preservationist, rest in peace, but I was feeling pretty good about the Morgue Report. I thought this one was bound to make the top of the readership charts. It would get much better numbers, no doubt, than the piece one of Sarah's reporters did on how five city schools don't have any heat at present. Who wants to read about that?

—ᴍ—

I ᴛʀʏ Peggy's number. Awesome Dude says my mother is "out," but he isn't sure exactly where. One of the endearing things about the Dude, who is missing a card or two from his playing deck, is that he can't lie very well.

"Where is she?"

The Dude hesitates, then says, "She said I wasn't supposed to tell you."

I can hear a voice in the background that sounds suspiciously like Peggy's. She seems to be calling someone a bonehead.

I tell the Dude I'm coming over, and that she had better not be "out" when I get there.

That plan gets blown to hell in a hurry.

Not five minutes after I hang up, Sally Velez calls.

"You better get down here," she said. "The shit has hit the fan."

As indeed it has.

Sally gives me the short version while I'm trying to finish my coffee and get dressed at the same time.

We don't have a newspaper library anymore. We do have one "researcher" who is supposed to do the work of about three of our former employees for less money than any of them made. She's a good person, as far as I know. Being a researcher, though, she likes to research.

The story about that damn farmer and his damn cow out in Buckingham County has come back to bite me in the ass.

Terri the researcher apparently thought the story had worms. Three nights ago, she finally had time to go back and take a look at the date in question.

No farmer. No cow. No story. And soon, probably, no Willie.

Sally says the researcher went directly to the publisher with her discovery.

"Stine told me to tell you to get in here right now. He didn't look too happy."

No shit. This is not going to go well. I've shot myself in the foot before, which is why I'm doing night cops at the tender age of fifty-seven, but this time I think I might have eaten my gun.

There's nothing much to do but finish getting dressed, try to wipe the coffee stain off my shirt, and go face the music.

On the way out the door, I tell Butterball that we all might be eating cat food soon. She mews sympathetically.

This won't be the first instance in which I've spent quality time on the carpet of one publisher or another. Usually, I at least feel I have the moral high ground. This time, I'm standing in the pit that is reserved for journalists who make things up.

It doesn't matter that it was supposed to be a joke. I remember Walter Pines, who was an old fart nearly as ancient as I am now when I was a cub reporter. Walter got mad one day because the managing editor chewed him out for having a messy desk, which is requisite for being a good reporter. He wrote a funny little short about the paper's Clean Desk Club having a meeting the next Tuesday, hosted by Managing Editor Claude "Mr. Clean" Carstairs. He thought the copy desk would think it was funny. Somehow it got through everybody and ran in the early edition. Goodbye, Walter Pines.

And so, with the ghost of Walter Pines looking down at me, I stub out a Camel and walk through the lobby to meet my fate.

Sandy McCool, the publisher's executive assistant, greets me.

"What the hell were you thinking?" she asks in a low voice so as not to be heard by the boss.

"Still," she whispers, "it was pretty damn funny."

I walk into Benson Stine's office. He is behind his desk. He does not look happy. I suppose it is good news that he didn't have the guard stop me at the door downstairs and demand my company ID.

He picks up the tear sheet off his desk containing the offending story.

"I suppose you know why you're here."

I tell him I have a pretty good idea.

"In all my years in this business," he says, "I've never seen anything like this."

B.S. has only been in "this business" about a dozen years. I want to tell him to stick around; he'll probably see worse.

He calls Terri the researcher.

When she gets there, she looks very nervous. She can't be more than twenty-three, probably right out of VCU, and I'm not sure she realized the real-life implications of her discovery on the career of yours truly.

Still, I can't blame her. Actually, I compliment her.

"You did what you were supposed to do," I tell her. "You'd make a good reporter."

She blushes.

B.S. makes her tell us what we both already know, about her suspicions, and how she went back into the archives and found what wasn't there.

"I even looked a couple of days on each side," she says. "I thought maybe you had the date wrong."

She looks like she might cry. I tell her again that she did the right thing.

Finally, our boy publisher lets her return to her files. When she leaves, he turns the gun on me.

"What's amazing to me," he says, "is that one of our readers didn't catch on to this. I mean, don't we have any readers out in Buckingham County?"

I'm thinking not many, and still fewer who were alive fifty-some years ago.

"Out of curiosity, why did you do it?"

There isn't much reason to bullshit, at this point. I tell him I was pissed off about having another pile of crap heaped on my already overloaded plate, and I let that cloud my better judgment.

He adjusts the pencils on his antiseptically clean desk.

"You know this is a firing offense, don't you?"

Of course I do. Goddammit, why doesn't he just cut to the chase and do it?

I'm reaching into my pocket to take out my ID, ready to hand it to him, when he says, "However . . ."

The "however" is a pretty big one, it turns out.

Benson Stine prefers that we print facts in our paper, but he's no fanatic about it. I'm reminded, as my professional life passes before my eyes, of the little daily a friend of mine from journalism school used to work for. On its masthead were these words: "Truth in Preference to Fiction." Truth is good, in other words, but let's don't get carried away.

Two things saved my bourbon-cured bacon.

First, the discovery that our fine publication had run a made-up story would be a little embarrassing. We might have to admit that we don't have copy editors anymore. Maybe B.S.'s superiors at MediaWorld would wonder what the fuck their boy genius was doing with that rag in Richmond.

Second, and more important, the revelation that one of the Morgue Report missives was pure fiction might put the kibosh on the whole project, which apparently has been a gold star on young Stine's report card so far. MediaWorld likes it so much that they're making five of their other papers do the same thing. The past is not dead; it's news.

"Frankly," our publisher says, "we can't afford to let this get out. If a reader had called about it, or put it on Facebook or something, we'd have no choice but to fire you, which is what you deserve, by the way. But I've decided that we would all be better off if we just keep this to ourselves."

He assures me that Terri the researcher has been sworn to secrecy, although I wonder what will happen when, not if, they lay her off. Hell, I'll worry about that later.

I ask him if I'm still doing Today in Richmond History.

"Oh, yes," he says. "Forever."

It doesn't sound that bad, compared with unemployment.

"If you ever, ever do anything this stupid again," B.S. adds, "we will fire you and run a story on A1 explaining just what we fired you for. We'll even run your picture."

Fair enough. I actually thank him. I am not used to thanking publishers, not having had any reason I can think of to do so in the past. I know Stine is keeping his own ass out of the water, but if he throws me a life jacket at the same time, I'm good with that.

"And this was a one-time thing, right?"

I assure him that this is so. If I'm lucky, he'll never find out that the plucky paperboy braving the blizzard didn't exist either.

On the way out, he tells me not to expect any merit raises anytime soon. As if anyone in the newsroom has had one this decade.

Sandy McCool, who can keep a secret better than anyone I know, won't tell. When I get back to the newsroom, Sally takes me aside and informs me that the publisher told her to keep it to herself, and she's almost as tight-lipped as Sandy.

"I ought to kick your ass though," she says as I walk away. "He wanted to know how the hell this got past his editor, which would be me."

God, now I feel worse. Sally's been nothing but good to me for twenty-five years. I think dinner at Lemaire and a fifth of small batch Scotch might be the first step back into her good graces.

—⚂—

HAVING SLIPPED the surly bonds of joblessness, and with a good three hours before Media World starts paying me, I light another Camel and walk back to my car.

My little crisis made me forget all about my threat/promise to Awesome Dude that I'd be coming over to talk with my mother.

When I get there and walk in, the Dude is sitting in the living room, watching Judge Judy ream someone a new one.

I ask him where Peggy is.

"She said she had to go somewhere," he says.

"Where?"

"She said not to say."

I ask him if she's gone for a walk. No. A trip to the grocery store? No. Andi's? There's no answer.

"Thanks," I tell Awesome, who looks worried but is soon distracted by the judge.

Andi and Walter wouldn't be home now, in the middle of the day. At least, that's what I was thinking, but I see my daughter's car parked a few doors down.

She answers the door. Inside, the place is quiet, with young William off improving his mind in nursery school. It is inordinately neat, for a dwelling containing a three-year-old, a condition I attribute to Walter. If there were any neat genes in the Black family, my daughter, like me, did not inherit them.

"She's acting kind of weird," Andi says.

"Weirder than usual?"

My daughter gives me a punch in the arm.

"She's not weird. She's your mother."

"And your grandmother. What's she doing here?"

"I dunno. She called me at work and said she needed to come over for a while. I got away for an hour, but I have to get back soon. I told her to lock up before she left."

"Did she say anything?"

Andi shrugs.

"Not much. Just that she needed to get out of the house and could she come here. She hasn't said much since she got here."

She points toward the rear of the townhouse.

"She's back there. I think she's watching Judge Judy."

Andi has to leave. I tell her I'll make sure that either Peggy or I shut the front door on the way out.

Peggy has to have heard me come in, even with the TV turned up so loud the incontinence ad is hurting my eardrums.

"Mom."

She ignores me until I reach down and put my hand on her shoulder.

I ask her what's the matter, why she's been avoiding me.

She denies that, but then she says, "All this mess with Artie Lee, it's got me upset. Can't you please let it go? For me?"

I tell her how close I am to getting Eddie Shaw to flat-out admit that he was responsible for my father's death.

"That's nice," she says, "but what does it matter now? You're just stirring shit up."

I tell her that there probably won't be a newspaper story out of it when I'm done, that I've promised Shaw his name won't be mentioned if he tells me the truth.

"I just want to know what happened."

I think that surely by now her curiosity will be piqued and she will share some of my interest in getting the answer to a question I didn't even know existed fifteen days ago. From her expression, this does not seem to be the case.

The way she rises out of her chair, both arms straining as she rejects my assistance, reminds me that my mother is seventy-six years old, and a not-so-young seventy-six at that.

"Well," she says when she gets her breath back, "you're going to do what you're going to do. I never could stop you. Nobody could."

She walks toward the guest bathroom.

"I'll be awhile," she says. "Don't worry. I'll lock up."

I can take a hint.

I call Richard at the hospital to check on Philomena. He sounds exhausted.

"She looks peaceful," he says. It is, at this point, about all we can hope for, I guess.

I call the chief at headquarters and miraculously get through to him.

"I've got some stuff," I tell him. He agrees to meet me over on Grace Street, outside Perly's. It is warmer today. When L.D. gets there, he suggests that we take a walk.

I fill him in on what I know so far.

He nods.

"So you think he's going to tell you?"

"Hell, he's already pretty much done it already. All he has to do now is tell me who did the deed, and I'm sure I know the answer to that one already."

The chief shakes his head.

"What you've got to understand," he says, "is that I don't know any of this. You got me? Whatever you dig up, you deal with it however you want. But I didn't tell you a damn thing."

I again promise that this is how it will be. L.D. wants the light of truth and justice to shine brightly, but he doesn't want to be the one holding the flashlight. However this turns out, he figures there's going to be a dead black man guilty of killing a white cop and a civilian, and a couple of cops guilty of making that black man dead. The chief of police making cops look like killers won't be good for future intramural relations.

The chief just wants the loose ends tied up, and it'll be better all around if old Willie does the tying.

"Does this make you feel weird?" L.D. asks me before we part ways. "I mean, he was your daddy."

I shrug.

"I didn't know him. I never thought about him much until fifteen days ago."

I sigh.

"But, yeah, it's weird. How could it not be? But how can I not keep pushing now? I'm in too deep to turn back."

CHAPTER TWENTY

Thursday

When I got home sometime before one this morning, Cindy was waiting up.

"Well," she said, taking a whiff of my alcohol-scented breath, "how was your day, other than the drinking?"

It was, I told her, a date that would live in infamy.

—⚉—

Even in the fast-moving world of twenty-first-century newsroom clusterfucks, yesterday was one for the books.

At midday, it seemed like I'd done the dumbest thing a print journalist could do—writing a fake news story about something that happened fifty years ago and then letting it go into print.

By nine o'clock last night, Mary Louise Ferlinghetti had trumped my full house with a royal flush.

"How the hell did this happen?" Wheelie asked everyone within earshot after word got out, as if often does in a newsroom.

Well, Wheelie hired her, but nobody felt like mentioning that at the time. It would've just been rude.

In our newspaper's race to oblivion, the third major area to walk the plank after copy editing and our once-vaunted state bureaus was the features department.

Now that the department's former editor has been laid off, with most of her staff already scattered to the goddamn wind, we depend on freelancers for much of our light and fluffy content. They work cheap and don't get benefits.

As Mary Louise Ferlinghetti has so thoroughly proved, you get what you pay for.

The managing editor shouldn't have to spend part of his sixty-hour work week hiring a restaurant critic, but that's how it turned out.

Our last critic left on short notice when we cut his pay by 20 percent and said he had to start reviewing chain restaurants.

"I didn't sign on to eat at fucking Applebee's," was his benediction.

And so we ran a house ad in the paper and another one in the weekly entertainment rag. And it fell to Wheelie to weed them out and pick a winner.

He picked Mary Louise, he told me later at Penny Lane after his third Harp, because she had such sterling credentials. She had clips from two other regional newspapers, one in Wichita and the other in Milwaukee, that read fine.

She said she'd just come to Richmond six months ago.

"She said she moved around a lot because of her husband's job," Wheelie said, banging the empty beer glass down hard enough to wake up the guy on the end of the bar.

She was apparently charming enough that Wheelie hired her with only a cursory phone call or two to check on references. Hell, he didn't have time for more than a goddamn cursory call, what with having to put out a newspaper every day.

Things seemed to be going well with Mary Louise. I read some of her early reviews back in the late fall, and they all seemed to meet our plummeting standards. It did worry me that she gave Applebee's three stars, but *de gustibus* . . .

And then, on Wednesday, Wheelie got the e-mail. He showed it to me.

"You might want to check these out," the correspondent wrote.

There was a review from our paper, done by Mary Louise, and there was one from a daily in Phoenix. The whistleblower had helpfully highlighted one paragraph of each review in red.

The graf in the Phoenix paper described a particular entrée. It was a linguine dish with porcini-truffle cream and Parmesan cheese. The description made me want to run out and order a plate, and I don't know truffles from Triscuits. My idea of fine Italian cuisine is spaghetti Albert at Joe's. The description in our paper, which I had not previously read, was equally mouthwatering. Actually, it was exactly equally mouthwatering, since not a damn jot or tittle had been changed.

"Verbatim," Wheelie said. "Ver-fucking-batim. Who the hell knew you could even plagiarize a restaurant review?"

Well, it turns out you can. From what Wheelie said he learned in an intense conversation with Ms. Ferlinghetti, she was kind of stuck as to how to describe this particular dish. Apparently, in the restaurant critic world, "tasty" isn't specific enough. So she did what everybody in this godforsaken century does when they need help. She Googled it and found that, by God, an eatery in Phoenix had served almost the same dish, and it had been reviewed and oohed and aahed over by the paper's critic.

"A real critic," Wheelie said bitterly. "I asked her why the hell she didn't at least rewrite the thing, change a few words. She said she was in a hurry and didn't think anybody would notice."

We seem to have reached the point where doing bad shit is acceptable, as long as you don't get caught.

By the time word got out in the newsroom, Wheelie had already done what he'd have done before if he hadn't been juggling five balls at the same time. He called the Milwaukee paper and found out that Ms. Ferlinghetti's tenure there had been cut short. Guess what for?

"They said they wondered how long it'd be before she popped up somewhere else," Wheelie said. "God knows how many other descriptions she's lifted. We're going to have to go back and check every damn one of her reviews, maybe rereview every place she went to."

So, maybe Applebee's won't be getting three stars after all.

I feel kind of bad for Terri the researcher, who is going to have her hands full vetting every review our critic wrote.

"Shit," Wheelie said. "By now, I'm even wondering if Ferlinghetti is her real name."

You think?

As I was helping Wheelie out of Penny Lane, he turned to me.

"What was it B.S. wanted to talk to you about earlier today? He seemed kind of upset."

I steered him toward the parking garage.

"Nothing all that interesting."

—ɯ—

IT'S A teachers' work day, whatever the hell that is. Cindy doesn't have to be at the school until nine, which she assures me over a second cup of coffee can be "nine-ish."

She hasn't been out the door five minutes when I get the call I've been expecting.

"You wanted to talk? Let's talk."

Eddie Shaw promises me that neither his asshole son nor any of the rest of his inbred kin will be there when I come over to his son's house. I take him at his word, with the understanding that I'm out the door and on the phone to the chief if it even looks like chez Shaw is an ambush site.

I go past Peggy's place on the way there. I don't have time to stop and chat now, and I'm sure my old mom would just as soon I didn't anyhow. I wish she didn't feel so damn bad about what I'm doing, but it has to be done.

As promised, Eddie is alone when I get to his son's place. He says he's probably going to stay a few days more "not that I'm welcome or anything." He says he wants to get some tests done at the VCU hospital.

"Anything serious?" I ask.

"Who the hell knows? And you ain't exactly improving my health, either, with all your goddamn meddling."

He makes me promise, again, that his name won't be anywhere in whatever I write, if I write.

He's drinking a PBR. The sun is barely peeking over the Oregon Hill rooftops.

"You're so damn hot to know the truth," he says after a prodigious belch. "Well, here's the truth. I hope you choke on it."

—⚬⚬⚬—

IT HAPPENED on a Tuesday night. Eddie says he and his partner, whose name was Warren—"You can find out his last name, Mr. Reporter. He's dead as shit now anyhow."—had come up with the plan two days earlier. That's when they learned where Artie Lee was hiding out.

"It was way over in Charles City County," he says. "There was a cabin back in the woods, not far from the river. Swampy as hell."

They scoped the place out on Monday, and they came up with a plan.

"It might not of been the best plan in the world, but it worked, didn't it?"

They decided unmarked cars would be the way to go. They were a little cautious about driving up to the cabin, not knowing who or what they might run into there. They saw Artie Lee's car parked in the woods off a ways, "but we didn't know who else might be in there."

They also knew that they wanted Artie Lee dead.

"We didn't have no desire to have it drag out in the courts, maybe have some judge give him life instead of frying his ass."

Plus, there was the little matter of that rape thingy hanging over the heads of Eddie Shaw and his partner. He figured that my father might be made privy to that information by one of his old friends before the trial. That could make things a little warm for the two detectives if that bit of dirty linen got aired out.

"We just figured it would be better to do the Old Testament thing, you know. An eye for an eye, although we'd have had to kill your old man twice to make up for what he did."

I guess it could have been worse. They weren't too many years past the time when a black man who killed a cop and the cop's girlfriend would have been tortured and then lynched.

It was bad enough though.

They hit on the idea of a roadblock because Eddie's partner had read about something like that working in a book.

"Son of a bitch read all the time, cheap detective stories."

They staked out the place Monday night, and they saw Artie Lee leave a little after eight and then come back a couple of hours later. They figured he was going somewhere to get food from someone who was not completely opposed to killing cops sympathetic to the Klan.

"We thought he might head out every night, after dark."

The next night, the last one of my father's life, Eddie's partner was in place to set up the roadblock half a mile down the road, in the direction Artie Lee had gone the night before.

Just after eight thirty, Eddie, who was parked on a dirt path across the state road from the cabin, saw the car lights coming up the trail.

He radioed ahead when Artie turned the same way he had the night before. Then he waited a few seconds and followed him.

"He knew he was fucked when he saw my partner's car blocking the road," Eddie Shaw says, "but there wasn't anywhere to turn around. And if he had turned around, there I was right behind him. There wasn't any other cars in sight."

Eddie says my father didn't try to make a run for it when the two of them flashed their badges. When they put the handcuffs on him, Artie Lee just said, "Well, you got me. Do your worst."

By "worst," I doubt if my father was thinking of a quick little execution on a lonely country road.

They put him back in the driver's seat, handcuffed hands behind him. They strapped him in. They poured some of the fifth Eddie had bought on him, held his nose and made him swallow some of it, then gagged him and threw the open bottle down on the floorboard.

Then, Eddie, who had the keys, got in on the passenger's side and started the engine. He took the brick he'd brought and placed it on the accelerator pedal. His partner steered as he trotted alongside on the driver's side.

They had picked the spot because it was right before a curve and a drop-off to a creek feeding into the James.

"It was thirty feet down at least. I got in my car behind him and gave that Ford a nice little push, right over the edge. Warren had twisted the wheel to the right, and it went off that curve pretty as you please."

They went down the ravine just like they were investigating a run-of-the-mill wreck.

I'm not sure I want to know the answer to the next question, but I ask it anyhow.

"Was he still alive?"

Eddie Shaw hesitates, but then he nods.

"Yeah. Son of a bitch was cut up pretty bad, but he was still breathing."

Eddie took care of that.

"Hadn't ever strangled a man before," he says. "It was harder than I thought it'd be."

His partner took the handcuffs and gag off. Then they climbed back up the hill and phoned it in anonymously.

"Then we got the hell out of there.

"Nobody was all that interested in looking into it too much. We hadn't put it out yet to the damn newspapers that Lee was the prime suspect, so I don't suppose the general public gave two shits about some nigger dying in an automobile crash. Didn't nobody ask any questions."

The plan, Eddie explains, was to have it all more or less swept under the rug: no big uproar about Artie Lee being the one who planted the bomb, and no Arthur Meeks and Arkie Bright giving the paper some rather damning information on the sexual exploits of a couple of the city's veteran detectives.

"That's what that black son of a bitch, the one that caught us with that girl, said he wanted. 'Do what you have to do with Artie Lee,' is the way he said it. 'Just leave us the fuck alone and we'll leave you alone.'"

Eddie says the boy who apparently was out after dark playing, the one who said he thought he saw two other men around Artie Lee's car, wasn't that hard to convince that he hadn't seen anything at all.

"You shoulda seen that little nigger's eyes when we got him down to the station and started telling him all the bad things we did to little boys who told lies," Eddie Shaw says. He laughs and it segues into a coughing fit.

And so now I know the whole story, one I'm not likely to write.

One thing, though, nags at me.

"You never told me," I say to Eddie, who is lying back now, recovering from his cough but not looking so well. "How did you find out where he was?"

I can see Eddie Shaw's yellow teeth shine in the light of the screen on the muted TV set.

"Now," he says "that's a whole 'nother story. That's the one that's going to be my insurance. I don't trust your ass not to bust me, but this will make sure you don't tell this shit to anybody."

CHAPTER TWENTY-ONE

Friday

Philomena left us this morning.

I get a call from Chanelle not long after seven.

She says Richard wanted to let me know. I thank her and find out that the family will be gathering at Philomena's home as soon as they get everything settled at the hospital. Chanelle says her aunt "didn't suffer," which is pretty much what they always say, like it's supposed to make everybody feel better.

I promise to come by there before noon. Cindy advises me, when she learns about it, to bring something to eat, maybe stop by Sally Bell's and buy a few pounds of potato salad.

It isn't a damn picnic, I inform her.

She rolls her lovely, sleep-crusted eyes and wonders out loud if I was raised by wolves.

I'll miss Momma Phil. Not as much as Richard and Chanelle and the boys will, for sure, but she was one of those people who give you hope for the human race.

"I wish I could go with you," Cindy says, but school's back in session today.

The day feels out of whack already. News of Philomena's death succeeded a semi-sleepless night.

Yesterday, I more or less went through the motions, after my meeting with Eddie Shaw. I had to be reminded for the umpteenth time that the Morgue Report is a daily occurrence, needing my attention. As luck would have it, none of our residents was on either the sending or receiving end of a lethal bullet last evening, so the night passed quietly.

A couple of times, Sally Velez had to ask me the same question twice. The second time, she advised me to get my head out of my ass. After what Shaw told me before I left, the extraction was damn difficult.

When I call Peggy's, Awesome Dude picks up. I ask him if my mother ever answers her own phone anymore, and he says that she's "out somewhere." This time, I don't think even the transparent Mr. Dude knows where she is. At least, I can't trick him into saying.

There is so much I need to know.

I tell him I will stop by later. He says he doesn't know if Peggy will be home then or not.

On the way to Philomena's, I stop by Sally Bell's, just after they've opened for the day. The place has been making box lunches for Richmonders since God was in kindergarten. I miss the old location. Like all lifelong residents of the Holy City, I never want anything to change. But the potato salad is still what I'd have for my last meal. I think the secret ingredient is sugar. As Cindy said, you're always a welcome guest if you're carrying a tub of Sally Bell's potato salad.

There is time to run by Arthur Meeks's place and still get to where I'm going by noon. I don't know if Meeks knows everything I do, but it seems like he should be aware that, after fifty-seven years, we have the whole story. Well, I have the whole story. There's one part that even Meeks won't get from me.

Meeks answers after I've been knocking for about five minutes. He looks like he'd be just as glad not to find me at his front door.

He relaxes a bit when I tell him that I'm here to give information rather than to receive.

None of what I tell him seems to come as a shock.

"I knew they killed him," he says as he sits back in his favorite chair. "I didn't know how they did it, but I knew they did it."

I know the answer, but I ask him again if he's sure that neither he nor Arkie Bright told the cops where Artie Lee was hiding out.

He shakes his head.

"We didn't know nothing," he says. "We didn't want to know nothing. Shaw and that other fella, they expected us to give him up. I just told 'em that we'd already done everything except deliver him with a nice bow wrapped around him."

He leans forward and looks me in the eye.

"We was hoping he was long gone, because we didn't have any hopes whatsoever that they were going to let Artie Lee get his day in court."

Maybe I should feel resentful toward Arthur Meeks. Even if he wasn't the one who told those two detectives where to find my father, he did more or less seal his fate.

Looking at him now, though, and trying to put my size thirteens in his shoes and walk like it was 1961, I can't work up a good hard-on for Arthur Meeks.

We talk a bit more, and then it's time to go. I know I might not see the old man again. I wish him well.

At the door, he has the last word:

"Back then, there wasn't enough Artie Lees."

—〰—

It's not much more than five minutes from Meeks's place to Philomena's. I've left the potato salad in the car, which is colder than the inside of my refrigerator. The aroma makes me briefly consider buying a plastic spoon from the nearest convenience store and tucking into that five-pound tub. Thoughts of Philomena tamp down my gluttony.

I have to park a block away. If the number of mourners is any gauge of how you lived your life, Momma Phil takes the prize. People have put on their Sunday best to pay respects. They all seem to have brought food, the universal antidote for grief. The Sally Bell's offering is well-received.

Richard Slade is in the backyard, by himself. I have noticed, in the years since we became acquainted, that he doesn't like tight spaces packed with people. Twenty-seven years in stir probably does that to you. Plus, he's not the kind of man who wants people to see him crying.

I say all the dumbass things people say at times like this. Richard just nods his head and thanks me, like he hasn't heard the same platitudes fifty times already.

I tell him that he can count on me to keep Artie Lee's grave swept clean.

"I knew you would," he says. "She knew you would. She said she could depend on you."

This brings me as close to tears as grizzled night police reporters are supposed to come. After blowing up three marriages and committing a wide variety of fuck-ups, small and large, over the years, hearing that a good woman believed in me is a gift.

To take his mind off his loss as much as anything else, I give Richard most of what I know about how my father met his demise.

"So they just ambushed him? And they got away with it?"

I point out that, if Shaw and his partner hadn't done what they did, there was no doubt my father would have been executed by the state.

I have to ask him.

"Do you think Philomena knew about all this?"

He looks out across the chain-link fence dividing his mother's yard from the one next door.

"I don't know, Willie. She might have had some inkling of it. I know one time, two years ago, I went with her to the grave, and she got to talking about your father. She said he had done a bad thing once, when he thought he was doing a good thing, and he paid for it. I couldn't get her to say no more about Artie Lee."

So we leave it at that. Obviously, somebody was giving food to Artie when he was hiding out. Maybe it was Philomena. No matter how deep you dig, sometimes you don't learn everything.

—⚒—

THERE'S ANOTHER stop I have to make before I punch in at the paper.

When I text L.D. Jones, he suggests we go to the ball field at Thomas Jefferson High School.

When I get to T.J., I see L.D. perched in the stands, oblivious to the January chill. I make my way up and have a seat on the cold-ass bleachers.

"We couldn't do this indoors?"

He shakes his head.

"Not for this one."

"Are you sure you even want to hear this?" I ask him.

"Hell, no, I don't want to hear it, but I've got to hear it. And after I've heard it, I suspect I'm going to get a bad case of amnesia and not remember a damn thing."

He asks me if I've got a tape recorder on me. I'm somewhat offended. The chief and I have had our differences, but I've never sandbagged him.

It does drive home, though, what a dicey position L.D. is in. He doesn't want to be the one busting veteran cops for something that was done more than half a century ago. He's got to work with the rank and file every day. But there's a metal rod inside the chief's moral makeup that insists on justice, or at least resolution. We are on the same page on that one.

So I spell it out: how Phillip Raynor and his sweetie died, how the two detectives found out who did it, how the other two Triple A boys did a little damage control, limiting the carnage to Artie Lee himself, and how Shaw and his partner settled my father's hash on an abandoned stretch of Route 5.

L.D. does not seem stunned by what I've told him.

"I've heard rumors, whispers, as long as I've been on the force. I didn't know all the details, but that's about how I figured it went down."

He looks over at me.

"So I guess you're going to run this shit like it's the moon landing or something."

Not exactly, I tell him.

If it runs at all, I explain, it will have to be almost completely anonymous. I've already promised Eddie Shaw that his name won't be mentioned, and there are a couple of other parties who will be unnamed.

"But why?" L.D. asks me. "You do all this work, and you might not even get a story out of it? You know the commonwealth's attorney is going to want to

throw your ass in jail if you don't give up some names.
You've just worked your butt off to find out shit you
can't even publish. What's the goddamned point?"

I can't think of any other way to explain it.

"He was my father."

—ɷɷ—

WISHING FOR a quiet shift at the story shop turns out to
be, as usual, a fool's errand. For a Friday in January,
Richmond's criminal element is rather busy.

A guy is found dead in his car over in Gilpin Court.
Two idiots in Bainbridge have at it over a dog, for
Christ's sake. One of them said the other one stole his
pit bull. The alleged thief proved that he had Fido's
allegiance by successfully siccing him on the accuser,
who managed to fire off a few shots at his adversary
while the dog was gnawing his ass.

I got Peachy Love on the phone. She told me the
pit bull did more damage than the Glock did, but neither of the human parties seem to be knocking on
heaven's door. The dog's fine, Peachy said, although
he's in the custody of animal protection, which isn't
good news. Who the hell is going to want to adopt a
pit bull? I'd love to put some of these assholes who
turn innocent creatures into killers in a cage with a
few of their "pets." Maybe tie pork chops around their
necks as added incentive.

Between the human carnage and pulling another
couple of Morgue Reports out of my ass, I'm kept fairly
busy. There isn't much time to deal with the one non-
journalistic item in my in-box.

Sometime before nine, I get a call from Andi. She
tells me that my mother and Awesome Dude are over
at her and Walter's place.

"She's not doing so well," Andi says.

Thinking in terms of calling 911, I ask my daughter for a little more illumination.

"She's just crying, like nonstop. Awesome brought her over here an hour or so ago. I told her I'd call you, and she said not to, kind of begged me not to actually. So, of course, I did."

I don't know what to say. Peggy hasn't been Peggy for the past couple of weeks. This is a woman whose reaction to real or imagined threats, as long as I can remember, has been to fight like a damn tiger on amphetamines. Something's got hold of her now, though, that has her going into turtle mode. This is a tad scary.

It would be scarier if I didn't already pretty much know what has my mother so spooked.

I ask Andi if she and Walter can keep the two of them there overnight. I promise that I will come by early tomorrow morning and take them home, although Peggy and I might take a detour.

"OK," Andi says, "but tonight would be better. Try to get here as soon as you can. This is kind of freaking me out. And it isn't doing much for Awesome's mental state either."

"Eight A.M.," I promise.

I'm able to slip away not long after midnight.

When I get home, I discover that Cindy has reached a settlement of sort with her son.

Instead of letting him separate her from fifty grand, she's going to "lend" him twenty thousand dollars. This is twenty K more than a sane person would entrust to Chip Marshman, in my opinion, but things could be worse.

"Did he seem appreciative?" I ask.

"Not so's you'd know it. He said he guessed he could get the rest from somewhere else."

"Are you having him sign some kind of note or something?"

Cindy sighs.

"Yeah, I guess I ought to."

I suggest that that would be a good idea, although I'd bet another twenty grand that the check she sends north is on a one-way trip.

As she turns out the light on her side of the bed, Cindy asks me how my day was.

"Well," I say, "it was not without its adventure."

And then I tell her, because I have to tell somebody, what I learned yesterday, what I didn't tell Arthur Meeks or Richard Slade or L.D. Jones.

The light comes back on.

"She what?"

CHAPTER TWENTY-TWO

Saturday

Among the perks of our sixth-floor condo rental are the sunrises.

The unit faces east and south, so anyone waking early enough can enjoy dawn's early light. This morning, that would include me. That big red ball is just rising above the VCU hospital complex when I slip on my overcoat and head out the door.

It's still dark at ground level, still cold as a gravedigger's ass. I dodge a group of insane people jogging past me on the sidewalk in gym attire, some of them in shorts. The state of Virginia really does need to allocate more money for mental health.

I light a Camel and stumble to my old Honda, which pleases me by starting on only the second try. The trip over to Walter and Andi's place takes all of five minutes, during which time I realize I still don't know exactly what my game plan is. This is kind of virgin territory. Hell, it'd be virgin territory for just about anyone, I suppose.

I'm there at eight on the dot. Walter welcomes me in and thanks me for fetching my mother and Awesome Dude. I thank him for babysitting them. Walter and I have very little in common, I fear. The only time we've shared a beer (well, three for me and one for him), conversation was stilted.

He's a good man, though, and that beats the hell out of being a boon companion.

Peggy looks like she hasn't had much shut-eye. The Dude no doubt slept like a log. He's barely awake when I come inside.

My mother acts like she doesn't really want to see her favorite son. After a few minutes of intense discussion, though, it is made clear that she and Awesome have to come with me.

We decide that I'll drive them to Laurel Street in Peggy's ancient Ford Galaxy. I'll walk back later and get the Honda.

When we get to my mother's place, Awesome climbs out of the back seat.

When Peggy starts to open the door, I put my hand over hers.

"Uh-uh," I inform her. "We've got to talk."

She struggles, but I manage to keep her inside.

She makes a sound, something like a whimper, and sits back, defeated.

"Where are we going?" she asks me.

I don't say anything. I've only decided on our destination in the last two minutes.

—⁓—

SHE PRETTY much knows, of course, by the time I turn off I-64 East onto Nine Road. I put a hand on her shoulder, partly to reassure her that things will be OK and partly to make certain that she doesn't jump out and make a run for it.

By the time we turn right on Evergreen Road, she's sure of what's ahead.

The AmeriCorps kids and other volunteers have departed until the weather gets a little more agreeable for outside work, and Evergreen looks as woebegone as ever, choked in ivy and thorns. The sun is starting to peek over the pines now, although it's offering damn little warmth.

We make the right turn and then park the car just beyond Maggie Walker's grave.

I go around to the passenger side and open the door for my old mom, like a high-school date. I offer my hand and more or less pull her out of the car.

"I begged you to leave this alone," she says.

I concede that she did indeed do that, numerous times.

How, though, do you get someone who's been a reporter his whole adult life to look away when the scalpel cuts a little too close to the bone?

We trip and stumble our way down the hill to my father's grave, with me leading the way.

We stand over it, looking at the only thing left to remind us of that self-destructive race man, Artie Lee.

The plastic flowers are still there.

We're both shivering. I look over and see that my mother's crying.

"Come on," I say. "It's too damn cold out here."

So we go back to the car. I start it. The heater begins to warm us up a little. We sit there with the engine running.

I look over at Peggy.

"I know how it happened," is all I say.

"I know you do."

Eddie Shaw called her. I guess the bastard didn't trust me to keep his name out of this. He wanted to make sure by telling Peggy that he'd told me everything. But, the way she's been acting lately, I'm pretty

sure she already suspected that the cat, sneaky bastard that it is, was going to escape the bag.

"It's OK," I tell her. "You're my mother. I love you.
It's OK."

But it's clear that it isn't, at least not from her
perspective. She's been carrying this around for fifty-
seven years. Like a cancer gone into remission, she'd
managed to put it into the far recesses of her brain,
until Philomena Slade asked me to be my father's
grave-keeper, and I got curious.

"Just tell me how it happened."

—w—

I GUESS Shaw and his partner had tried everything
they could think of to find Artie Lee, with no luck.

So Shaw went to the one person he was pretty sure
could tell them where Artie was. He and everyone else
on Oregon Hill knew about the white-trash whore who
had screwed a black man and had his bastard child
and was living with "it" right there in Oregon Hill.

"He came to the door," she says. "It was a Friday.
I was trying to get dressed and get you to the baby-
sitter's. I opened it. There he was, wearing his damn
police badge, and I knew what he wanted before he
even said anything."

There was only one thing in the world that could
have made Peggy give up Artie Lee, the love of her life.

"He told me they knew Artie had killed those folks
at that Klan rally, that somebody had already told
them that."

All they needed now, he informed my mother, was
a little information.

"I told them that I didn't know where he was, but
they knew I was lying. Two nights before, he had

sneaked around to see me from that place he was staying, out off Route 5. He shouldn't have told me where he was, but he did. He trusted me."

She looks over at me. Her hands are shaking.

"You don't remember, I know, but he played with you some. You was just walking pretty good by then, and he chased you around the room, you squealing and him acting like he was gonna get you."

Damn. I think I remember that.

"And then he was gone. He said he might have to leave town for a while. He kissed me goodbye, and it felt like 'goodbye,' not 'see you later.'"

Eddie Shaw explained to my mother how it was. If she didn't tell them where they could find Artie Lee, she could be damn well sure that she'd lose custody of me. She'd be going to prison as an accessory after the fact and I'd be some orphanage's problem.

"He called you a little bastard," she says. "I wanted to scratch his eyes out."

But she knew he had her. She had to choose.

"You chose me."

"Nobody ought to have to make that kind of choice."

And so, as I had suspected and Eddie Shaw confirmed, the one who led them to my father was my mother.

"They said they was just going to arrest him, that he would get a fair trial. But I knew that even if he did get some kind of 'fair trial,' that there wasn't no saving him.

"But I didn't know they was going to kill him in cold blood."

Peggy said that when she heard about the wreck, she knew it hadn't been an accident.

"Artie didn't drink, more than maybe a beer now and then, and he was a good driver."

I have to ask.

"Did you know, before that, that he had planted that bomb that killed those people?"

She's digging her index fingernails into her thumbs so hard I'm afraid she'll draw blood.

"Not at first. But by the time he came by that night, I knew everything. I felt bad about them people, especially that girl, she didn't do nothing wrong except maybe a little hanky-panky.

"But he said he never had no idea there would be people in that car when it blew up, and I believed him. Artie was not one to take things lying down, but I'll never believe he meant to kill anybody."

I assure her that everything I've learned bears that out.

"You know what that son of a bitch Shaw said when he was leaving, after I'd told him where Artie was? He said I was better off without him."

And so my mother has spent more than half a century, much of it living almost within spitting distance of Eddie Shaw's house, knowing what we both know now.

I reach over and pull her to me. If there's a mother out there as good as Peggy Black, I'd like to know where she is.

CHAPTER TWENTY-THREE

I'm on my third cup of coffee when Sally Velez comes in a little past noon, looking hung over.

"Did you sleep here?" she croaks.

I explain, as best I can, what has had me going for the past three hours, since I left Peggy in the care of Awesome Dude, walked back to fetch my car and drove here. She already knows I've been working on something about my late father, but I spell out what I've got:

Two people, one of them a Richmond city cop, are killed in a bombing at a Ku Klux Klan rally Fourth of July weekend 1960. Unnamed sources verified that the man who set the bomb was one Artie Lee. Those sources told how the black community was harassed for nearly a year before evidence of the alleged rape of an underage African American girl made the cops ease up on the general black populace, in exchange for the bomber's name. Another unnamed source told this reporter that anonymous law-enforcement agents found out where Artie Lee was hiding. The agents set up a roadblock, ambushed him, and orchestrated his death on June 6, 1961. End of story.

There is a lot that I can't or won't write. I promised not to name either Eddie Shaw or his late partner. I am not going to tell the world exactly how a couple of unnamed law-enforcement goons were able to find Artie Lee that night. I owe Peggy that much at least. I won't drag the names of the other two Triple-A Boys into it. They will play the role of "unidentified sources" in my little tale.

"Still," I tell Sally, "it's quite the yarn, don't you think?"

"Amazing, if true," says Sally, always the cynic.

"You know it's true, or I wouldn't be writing it."

She notes correctly that I'll be hard-pressed to verify what I'm writing, if it comes to that.

"The cops are going to want to know some names."

Without mentioning my earlier chats with L.D. Jones, I tell her that there might not be as much trouble as she anticipates.

"Well," she says at last, "this is a hell of a story, and you're bound to be accused of making shit up."

She gives me a hard look before adding, "again."

Sally says she has to run this one past the publisher.

I ask if I can come along.

"Be my guest. I could use the backup."

"There's one more thing," I say as she starts to call Benson Stine's number.

She stops.

"What?"

"It has to run tomorrow, in the Sunday paper. On the front."

"Why?"

She certainly is entitled to ask. The layout for the Sunday rag is already set. Something important enough to be on A1 will have to be pulled or pushed to the inside pages. I'm being a pain in the ass.

"Tomorrow's his eightieth birthday," I explain.

"Your dad?"

I nod.

Sally sighs.

"Well, that is a hell of a hook. At least we don't have to worry much about art, since every damn body you're quoting is anonymous."

B.S. isn't in, but he arrives half an hour later.

We go up and explain what we're doing. I have to admit that this probably is the most unprofessional true story I've ever written, full of sources I won't reveal.

Since the unfortunate cow-in-the-pond incident, the publisher has not considered me one of his most trustworthy sources.

This story lacks the verification our fine publication normally demands. Sally tries to explain, with me jumping in from time to time, how this isn't your ordinary news story.

"It's like a nonfiction novel, or short story, or something," she says.

I cringe, because "nonfiction novel" is first cousin to "making shit up," and that's not what I prefer to do. But it's my story, and I want to tell it my way.

I think Stine is intrigued by Sally's spiel. He kind of likes the idea of getting outside the day-to-day, meat-and-potatoes, school-board-and-city-council routine. Maybe he thinks this will make his corporate masters at MediaWorld notice him, in a good way.

"If the authorities come after us, and they want to know names, you'll give them to them, right?" he asks.

"Not in a million years," I explain.

I hear Sally groan.

There is only one card I have left to play.

I explain to B.S. that I've been in private communications with someone very high up in the police department since I started working this story, and that he would like very much for the outcome of that long-ago double homicide to see the light of day, but without his fingerprints on it.

"He wants it known," I explain to Stine, who is trying to follow, "that nobody got away with killing a cop and his girlfriend, but he doesn't necessarily want to broadcast the names of a couple of law-enforcement individuals who basically committed murder. It's a lot less messy this way."

To my amazement, the publisher seems to be willing to go along with this. I think the whole cloak-and-dagger aspect gives him a bit of a hard-on.

He asks me to let him read the whole piece. He promises he'll make a decision "soon."

On the way downstairs, Sally mutters, "Can you believe we might get away with this crap?"

I send Stine the first draft, all eighty friggin' inches of it. Hell, the turn will take up most of an inside page once we get a photo of Artie Lee's grave and have Terri the researcher comb the library for a photo from the 1960 bombing.

True to his word, B.S. e-mails Sally half an hour later and tells her that we can run it, as soon as we check with our lawyer.

I'm reading over her shoulder, and we both groan.

The lawyer we have on retainer from one of the old-money Richmond firms is in the business of saying "no." He sees his job as keeping us from losing lawsuits. This is not a bad goal, but like anything, it can be overdone. A lot of good stories don't make it into print because newspapers, especially in their current straightened circumstances, can't afford to write big checks to aggrieved subjects.

To our amazement, though, the publisher calls Sally again. I guess he wanted to impart this good news himself.

"He said the lawyer was worried, but that he guessed the fact that we don't use the names of a lot of your sources actually works in our favor."

The anonymous can't sue. Hell, I hope that's true.

Mark Baer and Sarah Goodnight come over to see what Sally and I are so exercised about. I let them see the first graf:

> *Today is my father's eightieth birthday, but he's not around to celebrate it. Because he blew up a couple of people at a Ku Klux Klan rally back in 1960, he died young and violently. This is how it all happened.*

Sarah whistles when she's read the first few lines.

She reads a little farther and remarks on the fact that she bets I'll never get this past the publisher, with all the anonymous sources.

"Already done."

"Wow," Sarah says, "maybe our baby publisher has grown a pair."

CHAPTER TWENTY-FOUR

Sunday

The back table at Joe's is in full throat. R.P. and Andy are arguing about the relative merits of John Prine and Tom Petty. No one else seems to give a shit, but the disagreement appears to be on the level of Christian vs. Muslim for my old Hill buddies.

"How can you say that?" Andy asks, banging the table hard enough to knock over his empty Bloody Mary glass. "Prine doesn't sing. He croaks. He couldn't carry a tune in a paper bag."

R.P. replies that Petty couldn't hold Prine's jock strap, that Prine was a real poet, not just some damn singer.

Andy starts singing, to general chagrin:

"Listen honey, can you see? Baby, you would bury me if you were in the public eye givin' someone else a try."

R.P. replies with a few lines from some ditty about a guy watching headlights racing to the corner of the kitchen wall, whatever that means. At least he doesn't try to sing.

"The man is an artist," he proclaims.

Just when things are reaching the boiling point, the two of them find a common enemy when a couple in the next booth cast their vote for Joni Mitchell. Cindy sides with the strangers, while Abe and I try to keep us from all getting thrown out of our Sunday brunch hangout.

We managed to get all sides to deescalate. With nothing resolved, we turn back to our drinks. Our put-upon server asks us if we're "finally" ready to order some food.

The conversation turns to the story that has to be on everyone's mind.

"How can you run that, without using any names or anything?" R.P. asks.

He's talking about the A1 story, the one about Artie Lee, of course. Walking past the booths and bar stools on the way to our table, I count at least five parties reading either A1 or the turn page where the rest of the story resides. I'll bet this one even tops the Morgue Report on the online hit list.

I explain that promises were made. Cindy, of course, knows about Peggy's role in my father's demise, but I haven't even told Abe yet. Custalow is pretty observant, though, and it wouldn't surprise me if he's already figured it out. If Andy and R.P. know, they aren't saying.

Andy accepts his next cheap Bloody Mary and drains about half of it.

"But the guys, the cops who killed this Artie Lee, they're probably already dead, right?"

If I told you, I inform them, I'd have to kill you.

"Man," R.P. says, "and this guy was your dad? I mean, how does that make you feel?"

That would be a hard one to answer. I'm not too much into feelings. Cindy certainly can attest to that. She reminds me often enough about my propensity for not sharing. Maybe telling her what Peggy did that

Friday night in June of 1961 portends a more sensitive, sharing Willie. Or not.

It is weird though. I mean, Artie Lee probably deserved to have the karma bus back over him. No matter whether you intend to kill somebody or not, setting off a bomb with even the possibility of a fatal outcome is probably chair-worthy.

On the flip side, it was a Klan rally. There are those who would argue that anyone prone to wearing sheets, burning crosses and terrifying a whole race of folks might be asking for a little cosmic payback themselves.

My father's been gone almost my entire life. Since Peggy told me about it, I swear I think I can remember that evening when Artie Lee slipped into Peggy's place for the last time.

Still, the only thing to do about it now, other than indulging my inclination to put what I know (most of it anyhow) in the newspaper, is to be sure that Artie Lee's grave is kept clean.

The story this morning pointedly does not give very specific directions to my father's grave, lest some brave bastards want to slip out there in the dead of night and desecrate it. Whatever he did, he's my father. It's funny, but a part of me thinks that Artie Lee, wherever his immortal soul resides, is pleased that the whole world now knows what he did that day.

We even get a call from Goat Johnson, who reads the paper online in Ohio. When I check the cell number and answer, he wants to know the same thing everyone else does, and I give him the same answer.

"You know something," he says, in that loud, beefy voice of his, "I think I'd like to have known your old man."

—⟶—

WE WANDER out into the sunlight. It's supposed to get up to sixty-seven degrees today. You've got to love Richmond winters. Here today, gone tomorrow.

I pass on an invitation to watch the NFL playoff games at R.P.'s. It seems more important right now to check in on Peggy.

Awesome Dude answers the door and says she's "resting." The place reeks a bit of my mother's favorite mood-elevator and painkiller.

I find her in her bedroom. She's still in her night-gown.

I sit beside her on the bed. She moves slightly to make room.

"I'm sorry," I say. I'm not sorry for writing the story. I am sorry for the pain it's causing her.

She looks up at me. It seems like the first time in weeks she's looked me in the eye.

"There just wasn't any other way for it to go," she says.

I tell her I'm well aware of that. My thoughts turn to Eddie Shaw. I wish him the worst. What kind of son of a bitch makes a woman choose between her man and her child?

I tell her again that he was doomed either way, that she made the right choice. Even if she thought Artie Lee could have somehow gotten away, I'm sure Peggy would have made the choice she made. That's what I tell myself.

"There wasn't a day I didn't think about him," she says. "I tried. I burned all his pictures, and I acted like I'd never known Artie Lee. But he kept popping up. I'd have a dream about him, and it'd be with me the whole day."

"And you never said anything to anybody."

"Hell, no. That's the last thing I wanted to do."

She starts to roll another joint.

"I did go to his funeral though."

I don't say anything.

"They didn't really want me there, I don't think. I sat in the back row. The way some of them looked at me, I thought they must of known I was the one that told."

To make her feel better, I tell her all about Arthur Meeks and Arkie Bright, and the deal they made to save themselves.

Peggy shakes her head.

"I guess we all knew we had to give him up to save ourselves."

And me, I remind her. She saved me, too, from growing up in some damn orphanage.

"Yeah," she concedes, "there was that."

She gets dressed and comes out of the bedroom. Cindy gives her a hug.

Andi comes by with young William, who brightens my mother's mood somewhat.

Peggy has been through a lot in her life. She's been tossed out by her family for having a child with a black man, and then she lost him. She's spent most of her adult life working crap jobs to put food on the table and a roof over our heads.

What I am banking on is that she is too tough to let this fissure on the surface of her life do anything but steam for a little while and then recede back to the depths in which she has kept it corked all these decades.

Either that, or she can just smoke more dope.

We are about ready to leave, hopefully in time to catch the second playoff game, when my phone buzzes in my pocket.

It's Raymond Shaw.

"I hope you're happy," Razor says. "You've managed to kill him."

I find out, between curses, that "him" is Eddie. Razor's old dad isn't dead, but he did have a fairly major stroke this morning. They found him curled up in his bed, unable to speak. He'd probably been like that for some time, because the folks at the hospital didn't seem to think there was much chance of reversing it.

I remind Raymond that I kept my promise and did not use his father's name.

"But you got him so worked up that he had a stroke. I blame you for that."

Take a number, I want to tell the asshole. Most people don't want their dirty linen hung out on the public clothesline, even if the big world will never know who they are.

I'm hoping Raymond will calm down soon and I won't have to take out a restraining order against him. Actually, though, a little dustup with ol' Razor wouldn't bother me that much.

I do tell him that my sorrow over his father's stroke is diminished somewhat by the call Eddie made recently to Peggy, the one that really put her over the edge. Thank God or Lipitor or something that she didn't have a stroke too.

At any rate, there's little likelihood now that any law enforcement agency is going to come after me to reveal my sources. And if they do, well, I've gone to jail before to keep my word.

I do feel a slight twinge about Eddie Shaw's stroke. But I'll get over it.

CHAPTER TWENTY-FIVE

Monday

The grief is palpable. I'd like to rent out this congregation and this choir when my time comes. Yeah, I want people to wail and moan, not have some mealy-mouthed Presbyterian preacher say a few lukewarm words before the congregation adjourns for cake and punch.

As little as I deserve it, I want them to miss me when I'm gone.

Unlike me, Philomena Slade has earned this. She will, as everyone understates, leave a big hole.

The little church is full to the brim. Cindy, who took a day off from work, has to stand at the back by herself, because Richard asked me to be a pallbearer.

Then, two tearful, joyous hours later, it's over. We haul the casket out to the hearse and make our way to the cemetery.

The warm spell we're enjoying makes Evergreen seem a little less foreboding. At this rate, the forsythia will be blooming in another week. The weather guys and gals are practically giddy, making stupid-ass jokes about global warming, like a three-day stretch of January sweater weather in Richmond proves shit.

I'm sweating by the time we lug Philomena's final home over to the grave site. We are maybe one hundred yards from Artie Lee's stone. I'm pleased to see that the plot Philomena chose is out in the open, clear of briers and debris. I'm sure Richard will make sure it stays that way.

He told me he's planning to move into his mother's home now, maybe add an extra bedroom and bath. He has some money, compliments of the state that kept him locked up all those years. He has a lady friend, and he tells me she is expecting their first child. A wedding is in the offing. I tell him that the Blacks are expecting nuptials in the near future as well.

Richard Slade is fifty-two years old and just now really getting traction in the life he deserves, the one he had to postpone for so long.

He'll be seventy by the time that little fetus graduates from high school. He says he won't mind the extra work.

—✺—

My phone has been busy the last twenty-four hours. People who knew me from Oregon Hill have called, wanting to talk about Artie Lee, whom they never met. A couple of them even expressed regrets for not being kind enough to little Willie Black, son of an African American dad and a single white mom in Richmond's most redneck neighborhood.

I'm as gracious as I'm capable of being. Really, whatever cruelty might have been inflicted on me half a century ago has been bleached out long ago. Sure, I'd still like to kick Razor Shaw's ass, might do it yet if my fifty-seven-year-old body is willing, but Razor and his ilk picked on anyone who had a weak spot. The trick on the Hill was either to not have weak spots or do a good job of hiding them.

L.D. Jones called too.

"Good story," he said. I don't know if L.D. had ever said those words to me before. When he calls me about something I've written, it's usually to curse me or threaten me with jail time. The chief's idea of what the public should know often differs from mine. This time, rare as a blue moon, our wishes have coincided.

I check with my reliable source at the hospital and find out that Eddie Shaw died during the night. It would be hypocritical of me to mourn his passing.

And I hear from Arthur Meeks. He read the story and mostly liked it.

His only beef:

"You said them two 'anonymous' sources was now elderly. Hell, I ain't elderly. I'm old, but I ain't elderly."

I apologize for my mischaracterization.

He accepts my apology.

"You know," he says, "this has got me thinking about Artie Lee. Me and Arkie Bright, he came to visit me the other day. I guess this has kind of brought us back together after all these years. And we decided we want to visit out there where he's buried."

In addition to the Artie Lee story and my usual crime-centric and historical offerings, I did find time to write another piece for the weekend editions.

It took a little arm-twisting, but I convinced Wheelie that Philomena Slade was well worth one of our special obits, the ones you don't have to pay for. I'd like to think that our readers, the ones who peruse the obituary pages, are wishing they'd known Momma Phil.

—〰—

AND SO, after we've finished singing and praying and have put Philomena Slade's body into the cold, cold ground of Evergreen Cemetery, most of the crowd makes its slow way back to Nine Mile Road and their homes.

Only three of us remain. Arthur Meeks and Arkie Bright didn't make it to the funeral, but I told them if they could come by for the burial, I'd take them to Artie's grave, which they might not have seen since his funeral in 1961.

Arkie says he drove them here. To see the two of them, you'd quake at the thought of either one of them out on Interstate 64. They seem to be helping each other along, Arthur with his walker and Arkie with his cane.

I wonder if we'll make it down to Artie Lee's grave site, but finally, after a couple of near-falls, we do.

"Well," Arkie says, "it ain't much, but at least it's here."

They talk about old aunts and uncles and grand-parents whose wooden or crude stone markers are lost to time somewhere in the Evergreen wilderness.

"We ought to come out here and clean this place up," Arthur says, leaning on the walker.

I am sure that Philomena Slade, somewhere, appreciates the sentiment, as does Artie Lee.